I0533771

Seasons in the Dark

Seasons in the Dark

An Anthology for Believers Struggling
with Depression and Anxiety

CHRIS LEE

RESOURCE *Publications* · Eugene, Oregon

SEASONS IN THE DARK
An Anthology for Believers Struggling with Depression and Anxiety

Copyright © 2025 Chris Lee. All rights reserved. Except for brief quotations in critical publications or reviews, no part of this book may be reproduced in any manner without prior written permission from the publisher. Write: Permissions, Wipf and Stock Publishers, 199 W. 8th Ave., Suite 3, Eugene, OR 97401.

Resource Publications
An Imprint of Wipf and Stock Publishers
199 W. 8th Ave., Suite 3
Eugene, OR 97401

www.wipfandstock.com

PAPERBACK ISBN: 979-8-3852-6090-4
HARDCOVER ISBN: 979-8-3852-6091-1
EBOOK ISBN: 979-8-3852-6092-8

VERSION NUMBER 111125

Scripture quotations taken from The Holy Bible, New International Version®, NIV®. Copyright © 1973, 1978, 1984, 2011 by Biblica, Inc.™ Used by permission of Zondervan. All rights reserved worldwide. www.zondervan.com. The "NIV" and "New International Version" are trademarks registered in the United States Patent and Trademark Office by Biblica, Inc.

Scripture quotations from the Good News Translation (GNT) Copyright © 1992 American Bible Society. Used by permission.

Contents

Seasons come and go, they say,
But the rain soaks deep, the harrowing gray.
I curl inwards, fold against the fray.
The skies press heavy, like heart, they cave.
The winter rains. The winter reigns.

1

Wastelands

I DON'T KNOW IF I slept at all. I certainly got no rest. The door is closed and the bedroom is dark. My eyes feel like bricks that are crusty with clay and my brain is already traveling at the speed of light, throwing a myriad of thoughts at me like waves in a storm and there is no way I can catch them or hold on. I have no chance. I sink in them and drown. My soul groans.

Why are the covers such a refuge? They are like a lead cape I put on to protect me from the harmful X-rays of the world that buffet me from all sides. How I long for their protection continuously. I could stay here endlessly, safe from the world.

I do get up. I am barely able. Everything is heavy, like there is a thick fog that rests on me and dampens everything it touches, weighing down even the slightest of movements. That I can hide my weakness at this point and rise amidst it, for that I am thankful, but it is hard, and I feel like I am rising to stand before a firing squad. If I just go through the motions, I might be able to get the kids off to school before I roll into a corner somewhere, adopt a fetal position, and see how that works in the tuning out that I so need. It is my unintentional and uninvited "go-to." It calls inexorably. At some point I know I will find myself fired upon with such intensity that I will no longer be able to stand. It seems the imminent, lifeless crumbling is inevitable.

I make a coffee and focus on the shape I'll cut the sandwiches into so I can try to drown out the shouting of "*I can't do this!*" in my head that screams louder than the kids yelling "Don't touch me" to each other and storming through the house. They are the closest to me and yet they have no idea of this darkness in my soul. I am alone.

I whisper a desperate prayer and try to get us moving. I will fight for them. Perhaps they will not have to deal with the same battles as I have, if I can only keep fighting. I honestly do not know if I can. I did not sign up for this. I have to tell my legs to move, one in front of the other, and it's hard—I feel like I am trudging through mud. My phone goes flat as I pick it up to check the time and I nearly burst into tears. Nobody wants to do anything. Not the kids, not my phone, and not my legs.

The continuous sound of shell fire through the night ruled out any chance of rest I may have had. When I enlisted, I did not envision this full-scale war—it's not what I thought I was signing up for. I am sure that no amount of time in this hellhole would ever get me accustomed to the horrors. I try to block them out, think about who I'm fighting, that there is an enemy that needs to be crushed for our survival. That is the nature of war. I am tired and sometimes I must silence the voice that says "I can't do this."

I cannot even find comfort in sleep. Rest is fleeting, perhaps a couple of hours at a time if I am lucky. A three-foot-wide and four-foot-deep piece, dug into the side of the trench, with a blanket hung down to protect me from the wind and cover me so I can light my candle and write home; this is my haven, my only place of solace, but it is dark and cold. The lighting of my candle makes me feel a little warmer. What a difference the light makes, and yet my safe place is a dirty, uncomfortable hole. I can't fathom. At least it is raised and out of the mud that I have to trudge through every day. Sometimes the trench is filled with water and the battle becomes to keep the important things dry; food, weapons—not possible. It seems the enemy is often more than the Boches on the other side of no-man's-land.

Adrenaline works wonders in staving off tiredness, but it comes in fits and bursts. On sentry duty I need all the awareness I can muster as I stand on the fire step for stand-to in anticipation of enemy attack. I stand like a statue, wondering if I can get my legs to move at all once I'm called on. Am I running to my death? As I stand there, I know the enemy is planning my demise. Even when his bullets are silent, his presence is ominous. It is like he has cast his fishing hook into the foggy mire and snagged me. He reels me in, pulling and straining with only minute rests in between, and there's nothing I can do. Surely there will come a time when I will fall. The death around me shouts of my own inevitable crumbling in lifelessness.

They have taken to mounting their attacks at night, of course with the support of covering artillery fire. The fact that I am aware of their tactics in using the cover of darkness does not give me any more ability to perceive them or protect myself from them. Their attacks work best when we are unaware, unready. I try to remain vigilant as best I can, but they are cunning, focusing on anything they perceive to be a weak point, and using high-ranking intelligence officials to strategize and bring us down at the slightest opportunity.

At times I feel useless. The training did not prepare me for this reality. The noise, the fear, the solitude. Even amongst my comrades my mind shouts at me that I am a million miles from home, and loved ones have no idea of the darkness I'm in or if I'm alive or dead.

4

It takes me forever to get out of the car once I've dropped the kids off and come home. It's those same old stubborn legs that refuse to move. I lean my head back on the car's headrest and close my eyes. I could go to sleep right here but I know I'm not tired, despite the sleeplessness. It is just somewhere to run to.

The gray in my eyelids draws my attention. I know I'm avoiding the things that need to be done but I still haven't been able to mute the voice that's shouting "I can't do this!" I'm not sure it ever goes away. It's relentless. Its presence is ominous and overpowering. I know there's a part of me that wants to fight it; that's why I can still move around every day and no one knows what's going on. My actions disguise the battle within. The battlefield shrouded in darkness. My enemy relentlessly attacking at the slightest opportunity, taking advantage of my weaknesses and proclaiming his victory in acquiescence with my inabilities. I am not prepared for this and my uselessness shrieks in intimidating consistency.

I head inside and down some pills to dull my throbbing head. It's all too normal to feel this way and I wonder if I ever knew a day where my head was free from hammers and knives. I have a vague recollection of not being in this war, of some degree of freedom, but it was so long ago. I manage to move with the intention of getting some housework done. It's slow and causes me to breathe deeply as I resolve to achieve something, but the goal is quickly kicked to the curb as I spot a tissue on the rug and it becomes in my mind like a mine ready to explode. I cannot even approach it for fear of the impending explosion. I stare at it for what seems like forever before dropping prostrate to the floor in tears knowing that I cannot pick it up. It has won. My fragility screams at me and I cover my head, but the voices are not silenced. My mind cries out so loud I think it could almost be audible, "It's too much!"

I lie there for what feels like half the day, though I know it's not really that long. Time is my enemy just like everything else. I eventually push up to my hands and knees and slowly raise myself, but I turn away from the tissue. Its defeat of me is too overwhelming. It is an anchor that I cannot lift and if I try, it will drag me along with it to the bottom of the ocean.

I have one last ounce of "try" in me for the time being and I move to the kitchen.

A barrage of bullet fire suddenly attacks as I pour some dry cat food into the cat's bowl and I freeze halfway down like a robot with deadened battery. The smell of the remaining tinned cat food in the bowl fills my nostrils and for a split second I realize that the offensive odor is something I've become accustomed to. How many more odors are wafting around in my life and I am too accustomed to them to clear the air? My mind turns back to my current battle and I wonder if I have any armor available, any ammo to fight back with. My delay is too long, the bullets hit their mark at full speed, and once again I sink to the floor. The groaning of my soul leaves me empty, and the voices echo in the hollow. "My life is worth nothing . . . Nobody knows . . . I can't . . . It's too much . . . I'm so useless . . . How can I stand? What can I do? Where can I run to?"

The refuge of the bed covers call and I somehow manage to crawl to their shelter and curl up in their enclosing atmosphere. The fact that I cannot even walk does not escape me and I groan at how pathetic and wretched I am. How long must each day be like this? Is there an end in sight?

I lean my back against the dirty trench wall and close my eyes as a barrage of fire intensifies and the volume sends my head into a spin. My mind is assailed with an intense feeling of terror and I can't escape the images in my head of the brutal fatalities I have seen over the last few days. I breathe in, and the rank odors of gun powder, human excrement, damp rotting clothes, and rotting bodies that have become all too familiar switch my consciousness from sound to smell and I wonder how I ended up here in this foul cesspit of waste and death.

The enemy roars at my subconscious that I am about to die, and my life is worth nothing. The battle around me thunders but for the moment is eclipsed by the battle within my mind. "What am I doing here? I can't do this . . . Where can I run?"

I am a soldier and I must fight; on both fronts.

Sometimes I have the vague feeling that there's advancement, that the war is being won. There have been rumors amongst the Tommies of victory, but we still know there's a timeline to walk. While the enemy fires, our lives are at risk. Some of the lads have had short breaks in Paris; I haven't earned mine yet. Perhaps there are some pleasures still to be had in this life, but they are not deep. The vague sense of hope that either break or total war's end instills, helps to keep us going, but I cannot imagine being able to function normally on a break while my head is full of those images; wounded, bloody flesh, faces blown off by shrapnel, and bodies with limbs detached and hollow eyes. Too many have lost their battle. Even those stretchered away to hospital may not be better off. It is more than just the destructive weapons that have devastating effect, and even with my body whole, my mind understands their suffering. The weight on my shoulders is oppressive and the macabre images are sealed in my mind. The heaviness threatens to force me to my grave with no redemption.

Tomorrow, I leave the trench as part of our usual rotation and then I will see how a change affects these thoughts. I will be sent to the communication sector five rows back, which will offer some relief from the onslaught for a while. A small refuge in a great war. How quickly we have forgotten the freedom from which we have come and for which we fight. Perhaps only those left behind will get to enjoy it. I will fight for them.

I wake after a short sleep, which was my only escape, and I realize that sometimes the accusing voices in my head do stop in favor of complete silence and darkness. It is then that I am overwhelmed with the sheer weight that pushes me down. The physical sensation of force, burden, and even implosion are all too real and sometimes I feel I can barely breathe.

I force myself to inhale deeply and exhale slowly. I cannot give in. I roll over and my flailing arm lands on the sleeping cat. He shrieks and runs from the room. I smirk. It is a rare occasion that any type of smile finds its way onto my face, but it doesn't run deep. I consider that maybe there are some pleasures in life, but I don't know where to find them. The sun gleams through the gap in the closed blinds and again I vaguely consider this thing called hope. Why am I in such a pit, looking only at the sunlight from the darkness? I have no strength or ability to pull myself into the warmth of its rays. There is just continuous, monotonous bleak and gloom. On the outside, I know others carry on with their lives as though they know nothing of the darkness and battlefield. They skirt the perimeter and seem at no risk of falling, oblivious and aloof. I continue to dwell in this land alone and afraid, stuck in this deep hole, and I cannot climb out. Life beyond this trench is just a dream.

It is time for me to move again. Once again, I am thankful that I can sit up. The yearning to stay exactly where I am is so strong, it pulls like a magnet, and the resistance I manage to muster is draining. This vague thankfulness strikes me as something positive and once again I grin as I rise. I sigh. I go to the window to raise the blinds and the sunlight bursts into my face. I squint and turn away as I consider that perhaps perspective and positioning have something to do with being found in the light. I look at the bed where a moment ago I lay in darkness, now shining in dust-filled beams. What a difference the light makes. Perhaps I don't have to do anything myself, or even move to find the warmth and life of light; perhaps it will shine on me where I lay. There *is* hope in that: if I don't have to rely on my own strength or movement. Could it be possible that there have been times when the light has shone on me—but I have been so deeply tucked into my perceived safety in the darkness, which I rely on so much—that I have missed it? That if I could only throw off the covers and come into the open, I would be found in the light? My mind whirs in endless circles.

This battlefield is a hard place to live in. The onslaught of the enemy is fierce and feels relentless. Even when there is a lull there is no comfort. Even the refuge is a cold and lonely place. It saps my strength to feel that I forever have to fight. I am drained by not even knowing what I will face from moment to moment. The voices, the pressure, the degradation and hollowness are all weapons that have catastrophic effect. For some, the battle is harder than it is for me; I understand them. Some are hospitalized, some have not been able to continue the fight. Daily there are reports of those lost in this battle. The recognition that I have not yet been pulled down to the grave beyond redemption doesn't mean I am better able to cope; it doesn't make me brave . . . or proud. It only means that I feel for them. If only the blinds would open and shine on them in their darkness. If only they knew there was sunlight out the window. I don't even know if I know myself, even as I look at it. Hope deferred . . .

This journey scatters thoughts like shrapnel, wounding every place they touch. I can't imagine healing. I don't know what lies ahead for me.

Gathering in the predawn and taking my place on the fire step for morning hate is something I put my whole heart into, knowing I am leaving the firing line today and that Fritz has robbed me of far too many things: joy, freedom, the comfort of home . . . my mates. He steals, kills, and destroys. The destruction is deep and total. I can't imagine healing. The early morning has been shrouded in fog. I am cold and wet and blind. They could be storming the trenches now. I carry the realization that added vigilance is necessary when the enemy is potentially so close. I do not know his next move. I know he attacks ferociously with machine gun fire from time to time and all I can do is shelter. We sometimes gain some ground when we go over the top but there are so many losses. Fighting fire with fire will not end the war. I can only see the death this ends in. There is only desolation and anguish. Life beyond the trench is just a dream.

If my rounds can reach the enemy and take some down, some of us may be a little safer. I have seen men stretchered away every day, some with horrific wounds. I have seen men fallen, their fight over. They are the same as me: loved ones unknowing, alone, uncertain. I don't know what lies ahead for me.

The routine of the frontline allows me to maneuver robotically and try to ignore the continuous onslaught in my mind. It serves to make things feel normal in a short amount of time, but I rue the thought that this is normal: that this is just the way things are from now on; continuous fighting, continuous loss, continuous death. Marching on in the face of annihilation, reserves of courage running low; where can we go to fill our tanks?

Our bread has been rationed again but I manage to have some pozzy and biscuit for breakfast before weapon cleaning and inspection. The officer sends me on my transfer, and I solemnly walk the two hundred yards to the adjoining trench where I will be supporting the transport of men, equipment, and supplies. My feet are soaked and aching, and I watch them as they move methodically away from the firing line. I pass many as they transfer back to the line. The enemy is indiscriminate; he seeks to destroy all. That I have made it out alive thus far . . . I am one of the fortunate few.

I don't know if it is in my head or the new position I now find myself in. The perspective is different. The officers around me have an incredulous smile on their faces and they are acting like men catching up on news in a saloon, not facing the serious matters of war. There is a joviality I have been unfamiliar with for what feels like forever. It is out of place in this trench, but I want to reach out and grab it like a long-lost child and never let it go. I go immediately to report to the commanding officer, but he only allows my initial introduction before shaking me by the shoulders and grabbing a telegram from the captain standing beside him. Everything feels like it is in slow motion.

He reads the beginning of the message. "Five past eight in the morning. Hostilities will cease at eleven hundred today."

He shakes his head as he smiles. "The war is over son," he shakes my hand.

I can't believe it. I don't say anything as he moves on to tell others. I think of those on the frontline right now, those I had just traded places with. That was not a good place to be: the enemy still firing. The news is being spread, I watch men go, but here we still are; in muddy holes, blown-apart fields, and ruins. There is no cheering. Images fill my mind of the horror I have witnessed; the war had been going on for years, and now over?

I allow myself to sit; nobody seems to notice. I am physically intact; for that I can be thankful. My mind perhaps not so intact, I will see. The realization hits me that I could go home, that maybe the healing process would begin this very moment. It seems surreal. The enemy was laying down their arms. There would be peace. I still did not know what was in store for me, but it was all that was needed to move forward. Light at the end of the tunnel. Hope and a future.

It was all I needed.

I collect the kids from school and continue on with my day as though nothing was unusual. They have no idea what a struggle it has been. My eight-year-old tells me about a mini circus act that visited the school today. Normally I have trouble listening, but their juggling feats and involvement of the kids enthralls me. It seems there is some normalcy out there, outside my hole, away from the firing line. He asks if I will come and help cut up fruit with the other parents tomorrow and I can't commit. That would be too much. I warn him with my busyness that he can't expect too much from me. I feel it is enough that I have caught a glimpse outside the pit. I have seen that there could be daylight after the endless night. Surely that is something.

The evening is filled with the standard chores and I find that tonight, unlike many other nights, I am able to complete the necessary tasks without collapsing. My celebration of that win makes me scoff as I picture myself on the floor and glance over at the tissue that still lies there.

I act robotically without putting too much thought into anything and it gets me through. It is exhausting though. I know the enemy still lurks around the corner, ready to strike at any moment. If there were to be a laying down of arms, it would be brought about by a power greater than mine. The kids smile as if they know something I don't, and I decide that I have to go to bed to escape their apparent ridicule of my condition. They know nothing of course, and I consider the aspect of perception and how what one perceives to be, is real to them. The knowledge does not free me. I send them to their rooms to read and quickly crawl into my regular haven. My mind falls to reflection again. If I don't have to rely on my own strength, of which I have none; if strength can be found outside of me, from a source that is faithful and strong, then perhaps there is hope.

I lie down, all too aware that soon I will rise again to start a new day, a new battle. The lights have been left on in the kitchen and I weigh up if I have enough energy to get up right now and deal with it. My energy is spent. My eyes begin to close; it doesn't matter. My breathing regulates and I realize I have survived. My pit feels a little less deep as I peer out over the rim. My mind whispers rumors of victory, but they are faint. I throw out my arm and notice a ray of light from the rising moon shine onto it through a crack in the curtains. A silver thread reaching me where I lay. A reflection of the greater light that will burst through with the dawn, a small reserve to fill my depleted tank. The bed is warm, the bedroom is dark. I glance towards the door once more before sleep will overtake me and perhaps tonight provide some restoration, none of my own doing.

The seam of light in the doorway remains. A bold thread, stitching the silence with hope. A way out.

It was all I needed.

2

Seasons

Seasons come and go, they say,
But the rain soaks deep, the harrowing gray.
I curl inwards, fold against the fray.
The skies press heavy, like heart, they cave.
The winter rains. The winter reigns.

My season lingers, no hope remains,
Echoing accusations, cruel decay.
Draught haunts candle, flame gives way,
Extinguished light, no break of day.
Oppressive weight, oppressive wait.

If voice could calm the raging storm,
A hand hold heart with blazing warmth;
Can light pierce walls, by darkness born?
The night, the cry, the hidden torn
This shadowed morn, this shadowed mourn.

Scarred battlefield, no victory won.
Dry bones lie still in silence clung.
The voice calls "breathe" in morning song,
Risen, turned home, new day begun,
The faithful sun, the faithful son.

Seasons come and go they say,
Darkness holds, like cold, like chains.
Yet light, though veiled, does not betray,
I will watch, I will wait
Not for seasons' end, but for he who stays.

3

Free for Freedom

COLD, ROUGH, HARSH STEEL; heavy on her wrists and ankles. Red, ulcerated, hurting skin, where the bonds rubbed incessantly. This was the nightmare of her reality; all she knew. The darkness of the damp, stone cell was all she could remember. Why she was here, bound like an animal in misery, had long ago left her thoughts. This was just life, if that is what it could be called. One breath in, one breath out, cold and dark and alone. Everything heavy, everything hazy.

She would turn in her seated position to ease the sores that had formed on her body. The length of her chains at least allowed her to rub her aching ankles and wrists in the tiny gap the steel cuffs afforded. She could at least wipe away her occasional tears, mostly left dormant now inside her after emptying her hollow soul of any hope that things could ever change. A heart of stone was somehow easier to keep beating in these conditions—why? She didn't know. She did not really want it to keep beating, but such was the lot cast to her.

Occasionally she would find a tray of provisions had been slid through a small gap along the bottom of the bars while she slept. She never saw them come. Her chains allowed her to reach them and she would struggle slowly to get her body to respond with the movement needed for their retrieval. The bread roll and water, stale and foul as they were, had become some sort of pleasure in her existence. There was a flavor in their foulness that reminded her of something from the past, more to life than what she was experiencing—something that her soul cried out for. The appearance of the tray was becoming less and less frequent, and even within her hazy thoughts, she marveled that her body continued with life even when it received so little sustenance. Surely death would not linger long, indeed she looked forward to it, and in her time of deepest thought there was a slight gladness that she could still look forward to something. Occasionally, she would consider why her jailer would feed her at all. Surely, he must gain some sort of pleasure from her misery.

A small, circle skylight in the roof, mostly covered over by insects, let enough light into her cell for her to see the secure bars six feet in front of her and the concrete hall beyond. She tended not to look to the hall anymore anyway. Glancing there would mean awakening her hope once more. There was some vague instinct that there was more than this; beyond. All of that was hazy.

The existence of day and night was only seen in the changing hues of the skylight but she could not tell how many of those there had been. When she still had hope she used to look up and imagine shapes in the insects of the skylight; now they were just a blur. Where there had been insects dancing, now there was only death.

Today, as she looked up into the orange disc above her and slowly breathed in the stale air, a sound invaded her ears and she sat upright in shock at the unfamiliarity of any noise other than her own. Her pupils dilated and her feeble heart beat heavily in her bony chest. She heard a distant door creak and then footsteps. These were sounds so detached in her memory but in this moment they turned a switch on in her brain, and a thousand images of what this sound could mean came flooding in. Her breathing was shallow and she shuffled weakly back against the wall. Was this moment something to fear, or hope against hope, to rekindle that spark that there was good somewhere, somehow?

She heard new noises now. The steps moved on a little, then stopped. She heard the jingle of keys and locks turning, another distant memory of knowledge once held, a life once lived—elsewhere, another time and another place, she thought.

She placed each hand on its opposite wrist and nervously stroked the red sores underneath. Her chains rattled and she held her breath for a moment, wondering if the noise had given away her location to an unwelcome new menace or if she should muster her strength and cry out to be rescued. Instead she just sat and looked intently, with wide eyes, into the darkness beyond. Maybe it was just the first time since she could remember that her jailer had come with provisions while she was awake. If that were the case, would she cry out to him, would she rush to the bars and beg for her release, or was he cruel and she would be better to not draw any unnecessary attention to herself? Why then would the locks be turning? Her foggy brain collapsed in the downpour of thoughts and she shook her head in anxious, psychotic dread.

The footsteps, keys, and undoing of locks continued, and the sound of the steps drew nearer. She could not crawl back any further into the wall, but she pushed back against it with all her might as though she could be camouflaged like a chameleon, as though there was safety in its flat, cold familiarity, protection from whatever was to come.

A silhouette of a man appeared at the bars in front of her and she felt as though a bomb had gone off inside her. Any life remaining in her was now blown to pieces. Her face was deathly pale as her exploding heart drew all the blood it could to remain beating.

She watched with shallow breath, not daring to move a muscle, as he chose a key and gracefully, peacefully, unlocked the cell and slid the bars apart. Tears formed in her eyes and her body quivered as he took two steps nearer and she looked up in awe at a face which, although she remembered so little of the things behind these walls, spoke to her subconscious of love and kindness. He smiled down at her, and she thought she could just make out in the dim light tears cradled in his shining eyes. As he spoke she thought her heart would break. Too many years of solitude, too much emotion bottled up, too much fury and hurt and fear threatened by one look of love. A tsunami was moving violently in her soul.

"I have purchased the keys from your jailer," he said. "I have come to set you free."

A guttural sob escaped from the depths of the girl; she abandoned the pressure on her back from the wall and released her tense body as though her entire skeleton had dissolved inside her. She collapsed her head onto her knees and outstretched arms.

The man bent down with a new key and unlocked the fetters from her wrists and ankles. They fell loudly to the floor and the sound echoed through her pulsing brain. He wrapped his hands around hers as she continued to sob in her position. His warmth radiated through her icy hands like an electric pulse, but she could not lift her head to even acknowledge it as her internal tsunami raged, swamping her awareness. Eventually the man stepped back as she continued to sob. He turned his palms upwards towards her and waited silently. This release was almost too much to bear. The weight that fell from her as those chains hit the floor was deeper and stronger than the mere sensation of heaviness gone from her wrists. A demolition ball had been chained to her heart and it had disintegrated at the turn of those keys. There was lightness in liberty. She was swept away.

The man stepped further back out of the cell and into the shadows of the hallway. In the back of her mind she heard his invitation to "come" but she was so overwhelmed. She knew she would race after him in an instant but as she lifted her head and ran her free hands over her naked wrists, her mind exploded again. She cried . . . and laughed. She hadn't thought there could still be so many tears left inside her. The well had been unstopped. "I am free," she whispered as she immediately forgot the invitation that had echoed in the darkness. She ran her hands over her ankles and pushed back against the stone wall to raise her feeble body from the ground. She stood weakly, still whimpering, and, supporting her body on the wall, raised her arms slowly in the air. "I am free!" she yelled, with the mightiest effort she could muster in her weakness. She sunk back down to the ground, exhausted, but smiling now. She looked around. Her old friend the skylight had new life and the insects within seemed to quiver with life; the cold stone walls were shimmering in her tear-stained eyes like curtains. The prison walls had been defeated. She sat for a long time, occasionally rubbing her ankles and wrists in disbelief, occasionally giving the fallen chains an indignant shove away.

Someone had paid to set her free, and now she was free. So this was freedom.

She curled up in a ball of exhaustion, amazed, overwhelmed, content, and fell asleep.

After the most peaceful sleep she had had in a long time, she awoke totally unaware of her new state of freedom. For too many years she had woken in a haze and lay in a stupor for hours. Now there was life tingling in her veins, and as she sat up dozily and reached out to rub her wrists as she always had done, everything came back to her and she muttered incredulously in a croaky voice, "I've been set free!"

Suddenly her brow furrowed with worry and her lips pursed. Was this right? She grabbed the cuffs beside her, carefully placed them loosely over her wrists, and stared in confusion at them. There was comfort in the familiar and an intense longing to stay with what she had known for so long. Her vision blurred as she stared and she sat like a statue for a long time. Eventually a single tear escaped onto her cheek and stirred her from her trance. She whispered again "I've been set free," and in slow motion dropped her arms to her side to let the cuffs fall.

She looked all around again, stood, and despite the pain in her body—happily, slowly—began to make her way around the perimeter of her cell. She ran one free hand over the wall and took each step with pride, her head held high and her chest out. This was freedom: to touch the walls that she hadn't been able to reach before, to move her feet, step by step, to choose which direction she would go. As she approached the open door, her hand dropped from the bars and she looked in front to the adjacent wall. She hesitated briefly and then continued her slow and deliberate procession, pacing laps around the room, oblivious to the open doorway, taking a wider gait as she approached each time to cover the span and continue her victory march of ownership around the cell. Free to move, free to stop, free to sit or stand. Gaining strength with each step but tiring as she continued, simply reveling in this new freedom. The length and breadth and depth of this cell was hers. She pressed her cheek into a wall she had not been able to reach when she was chained and coyly whispered of her freedom to it. She raised her hands and could just reach the low stone ceiling. She let her fingers brush tenderly on the skylight as though she had finally met up with a long-lost friend. "I am free," she continued to murmur. She raised her head to the ceiling and whispered to the bugs with a smile, "I am free." Freedom was pulsing.

She had not known this freedom before, she had been so accustomed to her bonds. She had been rejoicing in this freedom so completely, and yet now, as the thought suddenly came to her of the man with the keys and the sound of the turning locks she had heard, she turned to look at the open door. For the first time, the hallway beyond came properly into focus. As she pulled her thoughts together, she walked quickly to the back wall and sat down in her original position as she stared at the open door. She breathed deeply, regaining her strength, never letting her focus stray from those open doors and then slowly, deliberately, she rose and moved with trepidation towards them, grabbing the bars on either side for support as she finally stood in the open doorway. Her cold fingers gripped tightly as she glanced down either side of the hallway. It was long and dark, with cells on either side, all with open doorways. This was new territory, and the unknown beckoned. She suddenly realized that her freedom went beyond the breaking of chains. This was the beginning of freedom; there was more! She glanced back in to her cell. She could leave.

She had to leave.

With one hand still holding tightly, she reached out with the other into this new space. One foot carefully stepped out but still she feared letting go. She looked intently into the open cell adjacent to her. It looked similar to her own; empty, but somehow inviting. Despite the darkness she could see that there were differences and they cried out to her to be explored. They yelled into her consciousness that something different, something new, was what she was meant for. Perhaps others had been held here at some point. Perhaps there were stories the walls could tell her. Perhaps she would find a new friend in the crevices and mysteries. Finger by finger, with deliberate determination, she released her grip on the cell door and took two hesitant, weightlessly slow steps to the new room, grabbing quickly onto the bars on the other side as her heart raced, desperately pressing her body into the metal, anchoring herself.

Gradually, she found herself able to walk around this new cell and even step cautiously back to her own. After the initial fear, she now found herself overjoyed. Never could she have imagined such freedom. She smiled constantly as she moved backwards and forwards. She ran her fingers along the walls, excited by the different cracks and curves she was finding. She felt strength returning to her unused muscles. This movement was like an intravenous shot, injecting life-giving molecules of freedom that pulsed throughout her body, awakening senses and energy. To take this many steps, to feel the grooves of the new cell, to expand her knowledge and space, felt like she was taking tentative steps into the vast ocean, and finding the waves of freedom splashing her face and causing refreshment and vigor. Soon she found she had the courage to enter new cells. Each step became a little less timid and each was a link to more and more freedom. Now she was diving into the waves and discovering there was more depth than she could have imagined.

She found a tray of bread and water left in each cell, and though they were stale and foul as she had always known, this was like a feast to her that she could eat and drink whenever she wished. She would lie down and rest wherever she felt like it, each time closing her eyes with a smile on her face and waking still grinning with pleasure. She thought sometimes of the man who had set her free and inwardly thanked him for allowing her to experience these new places. He had opened the prison door and released her from her fetters; she thought he would be so pleased that she was able to enjoy this life of new experiences and opportunities, of being able to do her own thing, anyway she pleased.

It never crossed her mind that there could be more. So used to the chains had she been. She could have spent the rest of her days wandering from cold, dark, empty cell to cold, dark, empty cell and been happy. She thought she had found freedom in these cells; someone had set her free. This must be the purpose of it all. This must be freedom. She thought this was pleasure. At one point she found she was able to close the iron doors to her original cell. "I never need to go back there!" she said proudly and instead began to become accustomed to each of the other cells now at her disposal. She had never dreamed of the ability to move so much and have such space, but the one who had bought her freedom had other plans. Hour after hour, day after day, he waited at the end of the dark hall for her to turn to him, but she was so enraptured in doing her own thing, in what she thought was freedom, that she never turned in his direction, never even noticed he was there, waiting. He had even called to her to come after him, sometimes coming so close to her that she would be bound to look to him, but the darkness was too deep. She was still so engrossed with what lay before her that she would turn from him without recognition, as though he were a shadow in the way of her light. His closeness to her at times would draw thankfulness from her heart. Sometimes she would wake, remember the fallen chains, offer a whisper of thanksgiving, and continue to live in the darkness. She had not learned to recognize his voice, its gentle invitation unraveling like a vapor against the boundaries of her own making. She did not realize that each new space she spent time in was still a cell, still had bars and walls and restrictions . . . was still the domain of the jailer.

Finally, after days of becoming comfortable in her new freedom, her stores were running low and her hunger for more began to call to her like a little voice calling from the past, and she began to look further. She had explored the cells, and now as she approached the one nearest the end of the hall, she looked into the darkness at the end and recognized the man's familiar silhouette, etched into her memory after such a life-changing event. Recognition awakened now by need. Her preoccupations fell away like scales from her eyes. She let the walls crumble. She dropped to her knees in gratitude and clutched her heart as he took a step towards her. As he halted under one of the hall's skylights, she could see once again his kind eyes and loving smile.

"I set you free for freedom," he said. "Follow me."

He turned and walked back to the end of the hall. The girl sat on her knees, glancing after him. She momentarily glanced back to the cells she had called home and then leapt to her feet and chased after him. Where was he going? What of this place she had been living? It was time to give up this illusion of freedom and choose what really mattered. It was time to follow the one who held the keys.

She now saw, as she approached, that the hall ended in a darkened flight of stairs. She looked up at the man continuing on before her and began to climb after him. Her legs began to ache as she ascended; she wondered if this climb was necessary, if she should just stay in the comfort of her concrete walls and iron bars, but her aimless wanderings and rank provisions had inadvertently rebuilt some muscle conditioning, and she focused again on the man she was following, and continued to climb. Her weakness screamed at her to turn back, to give up the difficulty, at the very least—to stop, but she had seen his face; she had to follow.

As the stairs turned and continued up, she puffed and paused, pressing a hand against the wall to catch her breath. She heard the man's steps stop and felt a pang of panic—where was he? He was out of sight. She had to follow. Taking a deep breath, she climbed again, slower this time as her weakness began to speak louder than her will. It was time to pursue this man. Would he be gone? Had she waited too long? Could she finish the climb? Despair began to whisper as she looked down at her feet, desperately willing one foot after the other to lift onto the next step. It had only been a moment in her tiredness and downward gaze that threatened to overcome her, but the man had not left her at all. Right at her reach, and stooping towards her, he waited on a wide landing. She felt his fingertips on hers and looked up to find him smiling as he drew her towards himself and she fell at his feet on the landing. He paused as she raised herself to his side and caught her breath, and then he spoke softly, "I was always with you. But freedom is not found in the darkness. I have called you out. I have more for you than you can imagine." He threw open a heavy set of double doors and she fell to her knees again, bringing her arm up to shield her eyes from the blinding sunlight that streamed in and hit her like a hammer. "It was for freedom that I have set you free." The man stepped out and stood with his arms outstretched before her, inviting her to survey the wondrous panorama.

Beneath the shield of her arm, she could see his feet standing on lush, green grass, and she reached out with her free hand to touch it in awe as her eyes continued to adjust to the light. New tears formed as she felt the prickly, velvet sward before her. She began to sob and shake her head. What was this wonder? How could she have thought the concrete jail below was freedom? She suddenly was aware of the warmth of the sun hitting her hand as she touched the cool grass and the sensation, as well as the blinding vibrant green that she could never have imagined, took her breath away. She dared not even move her arm for risk of being drowned in the wave of beauty that she imagined was beyond.

She took some measured, deep breaths, gradually, slowly, moved her arm away from her face, and stood to look before her, still holding a hand above her eyes to shield from the brightness, the other arm reaching out to steady herself on the open doorway. She saw the man beckoning her to partake and looked around in wonder. Before her was an open meadow, lush with green fields stretching into the distance as far as she could see. She could not take it all—it was too much.

A wave of dizziness swept over her, and she thought she might faint. Then the sound of trickling water drew her attention, and she turned to see a small stream tumbling over rocks nearby. She clasped her chest as her eyes followed the river—and there, a table was spread with a rich feast. Hunger and thirst surged. Her head spun as the offerings overwhelmed her senses, and she began to salivate. The aroma suddenly flooded her awareness, but her body had no endurance left. The sheer magnificence of the sight engulfed her. She could take no more. Collapsing to the ground, she lay prostrate as sobs wracked her body. A cool breeze rustled her matted, filthy hair. She felt its clean, fresh power entering and leaving her lungs as she sobbed and felt that she could not take its intensity. The sun's warm rays kissed her pale skin and she wept harder.

As the sobbing waned she rolled onto her back and stretched her arms out wide across the grass. Life was real. It had been above her this whole time. She stared into the bright blue sky. The knowledge that this place existed—this reality—had been buried so deep within her that she had forgotten it entirely. She had been only too willing to accept that gray, cold walls were a measure of freedom. How wrong she had been.

She felt as though her heart could not keep beating. Despite the life, the breath, the exhilaration—the overwhelming explosion of true freedom and the exhaustion that bled her dry pulsed too fiercely for her to manage. If she were to be breathing her last, this would be the moment. She would welcome it; with this beauty all around her, with this man. There was nothing else she needed. Simply this savior who had been the author of it all.

She turned once again onto her stomach and peered off through teary eyes into the distance. She could vaguely see people milling around beneath the spreading branches of a great tree, and as she cast a sideways glance at the man with the keys, she knew instinctively that this was a further treasure of freedom she could move on to, as she was ready; that there was more, and he would lead her.

What a tragedy it would have been if she had accepted her prison cells below as freedom, thinking that just because the chains were loosed that she was living in freedom. She just needed to follow and step into the light. Free for freedom. Set free *to be* free! Not to remain caged and deluded. Not to walk into what was only another prison cell. The jailer had set these cells up to deceive, to make her feel like newness was freedom, simply because it was something she had not experienced before. But it was the same concrete, the same cells, the same bars. This savior had come to set her free for life, for breath, for love. He knew where it was to be found and it was with him! She had only to follow. Here she had found the way, the truth, and the life. Now she would live. Freedom was more than breaking the chains. He had led her out to bring her in, and she had finally learned to follow. She was free indeed. Free for freedom.

4

Overboard

The balcony bends, my perception,
My mind, death's inception
How long 'til my demise?
Deep waters beyond call,
If I jump, if I lean too far, if I fall
How long 'til my demise?

Orange glow of sunset mocks,
Creation's glory talks,
This beauty, not for me.
If I sink to the depths and darkness below,
Oblivion's host, descending slow,
That is the place for me.

Tears fall, crowd elsewhere,
My beloved too, away, afar, unaware
I cry aloud
If I don't return, they'll cry . . . then be free
How long 'til I'm just memory
I cry aloud

No one will see if silently I float away
'Til I tread no more, fall away,
Expanse draws
How easy to leap, yet static, staring, through drying tears,
If I do it, it is done, no return, vision clears
Still expanse draws

Invisible hands hold gentle, yet tight
Keeping me in place, silent might
What else keeps me planted.
Neither can I walk away from the balcony
Standing between me and the sea.
I am planted.

Is there any hope within, even shadow?
Void calls, Emptiness screams hollow
But still your hand holds.
Your love beckons. No one beyond reach
Nothing you can't change, unteach
Your strong hand holds.

In weakness, depletion, prostration, collapse
Heavy shadow, foreboding relapse
Held in your strong hand
No obstinate thrashing, no strength left, heart crashing
Surrendering to your bloodline attaching
Surrendered in your strong hand

Beyond the horizon lies a brighter day
With flower blossom and sun ray
To get there, move on
Lying in sorrow amidst the storm
There's nothing of comfort, nothing warm
Move on.

With what strength I turn from the beckoning depths.
That hand now guides, intercepts
I know not how.

The white peaks grow distant, Divine hands guide away,
Intangible solace for another day
I know not how.

Docking ship, masked joyful greeting, dry land no haven
The struggle still rages, abrasion
Yet something beyond is unseen
Beyond me, victorious mighty handhold
I don't feel, just numb, cold
Yet something beyond is unseen

No work of my own, no merit, no skill
No hope found on death row; still . . .
You hold
There in the darkness, in the fire, in the hole
In the endless ocean and depths of Sheol
Still, you hold

Is there any hope within, even shadow?
Void calls, Emptiness screams hollow
But still your hand holds.
Your love beckons. No one beyond reach
Nothing you can't change, unteach
Your strong hand holds.

Your strong hand holds

5

Psalms: A Reflection

THE WORD "REFLECTION" IN this context refers both to "serious thought or consideration" and to "the act of casting back an image or likeness." Both definitions offer meaningful insight into our engagement with the Psalms. On one hand, we reflect thoughtfully on the verses, particularly those portraying the life of King David and the emotional and spiritual struggles he encountered. On the other, the Psalms function as a mirror—casting back to us an image of ourselves as we encounter the stories and experiences of those whom God has chosen to include in the biblical narrative.

Through the lens of Scripture, we get to look intently at what life looks like when walking with God, and the types of things he permits, expects, blesses, and helps with in our relationship with him. One of the huge insights we get from these psalms is how to deal with emotions, which are God-given and able to be used in reverence and submission to him, to stir us and lead us and truly allow us to "feel"—as was God's intention. God gives us permission to walk through every emotion with him—and the Psalms help lead us through that.

In this reflection, we see ourselves in the joys, doubts, laments, and praises of those who walked closely with God. This reflective process and meditation deepens our understanding of who God is, and our relationship with him. We see him holding us, comforting us, being present with us through it all. The Psalms validate our emotional experience and model a way of bringing our full selves before God with honesty and trust.

Across the entire book, we encounter the full spectrum of human emotion, from the darker and more difficult experiences such as despair, fear, envy, anger, resentment, and hopelessness, to the lighter, life-giving expressions of joy, peace, gratitude, love, and hope. This emotional range makes the Psalms a powerful place for us to linger, reflect, and recognize that we are not alone in our inner struggles. It also reassures us that God welcomes honesty in our prayers—however raw or unfiltered. The psalmists never hesitate to pour out their hearts to God, whether pleading for justice, grieving over sin, or declaring confidence in the pursuit of God and in his faithfulness.

We, too, are invited to come as we are—to express freely what is stirring in our hearts. God already knows, yet he longs for us to approach him in truth and vulnerability, trusting that he will meet us in every emotion and at every turn.

Our ultimate cry for relief and freedom from our "negative" emotions and from trauma, depression, or anxiety, is to God. He is a good God. He is our refuge, our hope. His arm is not too short to save nor his ear too dull to hear you call (Isa 59:1). He can use whatever means he chooses to reach out to you, including other people, Scripture, praise, or even times of silence and waiting. Avenues like talking to peers and mentors and getting counseling not only help in support and guidance, but also help us to realize we are not alone and that others can relate. The word of God also has power—to, likewise, show us we are not alone, but to do so much more. It is alive and active and sharper than a two-edged sword (Heb 4:12), and it has divine power to demolish strongholds (1 Cor 10:5).

There are seventy-three psalms that are attributed directly to David, with Acts 4 and Hebrews 4 also referencing him as the author of Psalms 2 and 95, respectively. Many scholars believe that some of the unattributed psalms were likely written by him as well.

In his inspired word, God has given us the story and expressions of David. We see that even as far back as the eleventh century BC, a man of God—a man described as being "after God's own heart"—wrote about how overwhelmed with anxiety he was at times. In David's life, we see not only the support and guidance of God, but also David's wrestling with confusion, sorrow, and despair. The word of God does not gloss over pain—it gives it space.

If you don't know much about King David, I would encourage you to take a look. Even a rudimentary knowledge of his life can be helpful in understanding his cries of anguish found in the Psalms. His early years as a shepherd, Samuel's anointing of him as the future king, his victory over Goliath, his life in hiding on the run from Saul, his kingship, his close friendship with Jonathan, his sin with Bathsheba, and his repentance can be found in the Bible all the way through 1 Samuel 16–31 and into 2 Samuel chapters 5 and 11, with the end of his life in 1 Kings 1 and 2.

This "man after God's own heart" (1 Sam 13:14) still faced both intense internal battles and public failures. His story is marked by rejection, abandonment, and sin—but also by deep repentance, praise, humility, and trust in God. From the time he was overlooked as a shepherd boy to his anointing as king, God's hand was clearly on his life. Even when others saw nothing of worth in him, when he was told to deliver lunch rather than be part of a battle, when he was scorned and resented for his genuine actions—God saw the heart. To anyone who has felt unseen, undervalued, or overlooked and insignificant, you can be sure that God sees you, knows you, and loves you just the way you are. He does not look at the outward appearance; he sees the heart (1 Sam 16:7). In David's story, we see a man who experienced God's presence in his darkest places—when pursued by enemies, betrayed by loved ones, and caught in the consequences of his own sin. And yet, again and again, David acknowledges, even in those times, that God is his only refuge.

His psalms reveal this turning again and again to God—not ignoring reality, but anchoring his emotions and identity in the greater reality of who God is: his strength, his faithfulness, and his mercy. "The Lord is my rock, my fortress, and my deliverer" (Ps 18:2). This was not theory for David. It was not positive thinking, willing God's protection and provision into being—it was his lived experience, his knowledge of the Almighty, right in the midst of his troubles.

David's words are written here by the inspiration of God himself (2 Tim 3:16). These words are truth. These words show me I'm not alone; not only is God with me and hearing my every cry, but I can know that other people relate to my despair and desperation. Through it all, I constantly see that God is my source of help (Ps 121), the Maker of heaven and earth. For David, and for us, being in God's chosen place does not mean struggles will not come. Jesus said, "In this world you will have trouble, but take heart, I have overcome the world" (John 16:33). Though David be called "friend of God," though the Bible constantly shows him "inquiring of the Lord," he was not exempt from anguish and suffering. His anxieties did not automatically dissipate before full materialization *because* he had a relationship with God—but he presented them *to* God and worked through them from *within* that relationship.

My love for God and relationship with him are not negated by my anxiety; rather I have a source—*the* source—of comfort, direction, and answers, in the face and voice of the one in whose lap I collapse in utter weakness and pour out my soul.

He is my counselor, my comfort, my peace, my breath. And despite the reality—the tearing, ripping bite of anxiety or depression in my life—he is *greater*! He is *stronger*! He is *able*! He is the same yesterday, today, and forever (Heb 13:8), and remains who he is no matter where I'm at. No matter whether I am curled in exhaustion of weakness and inability, whether I recognize his Lordship and abilities or not, he is the same. He has shown himself true and faithful (Ps 33:4), and his faithfulness is a shield for us (Ps 91:4), and how much do we need a shield because these darts of the enemy can be relentless! The Lord's eyes roam the earth to find those for whom he can show himself strong (2 Chr 16:11). He will never leave me or forsake me (Josh 1:9). At this moment in time, maybe I am not an overcomer, I may *feel* defeated and failing, but my hope is in him—not me. He is sure, he is with me, even in this valley, this wilderness, this desert, going before and behind, ever faithful.

Recently I was considering the much-often-spoken-about biblical premise of "standing on the rock." David himself says, "The Lord is my rock . . . my God is my rock, in whom I find protection" (Ps 18:2). So many beautiful songs contain these lyrics which talk about being found on the rock: my feet are on the rock, not being shaken in the storm, etc., and they are so encouraging to think about the solid foundation of Jesus on which I stand. I was visualizing the scene from Matthew 7:24–27 in which the storm comes and washes away the house built on sand. I was picturing myself on the rock in that wild storm, being buffeted by the howling winds and rain. What I saw was that I was not actually standing on the rock. I was blown so hard and so fiercely that I had been knocked prostrate and was lying face down, with bloodied nose and bruised body and no ability to stand. There was definitely no standing defiantly in power, shaking my fist at the wind and proclaiming my victory. The strength was only the rock itself. I was broken, but not washed away. I had fallen, but when the storm passed, I would be able to stand again because the rock was sturdy and sure and enduring. My brokenness does not lessen the strength of the Rock. David also felt broken and weak at times; these psalms tell us this with profound honesty and depth.

When David was overwhelmed, he reminded himself of God's truth. He preached to his own soul. He remembered God's faithfulness in the past and allowed it to reanchor him in the present. His strength did not come from himself, but from the one in whom his soul found rest.

For emphasis' sake, I say again, *you are allowed to feel*! We all need the reminder that these words are here for a purpose—God-inspired! The Psalms recognize and make space for the full range of human emotion, including grief, fear, anger, praise, thanksgiving, and hope—and model how to bring all of it before God. They remind us that God is not afraid of our emotions, nor does he require perfection from us before we come to him. Instead, he invites us to come honestly, vulnerably, and often. Draw near to God and he *will* draw near to you. This is a promise (Jas 4:8).

These ancient songs still speak today. They give voice to what we sometimes cannot express, and most of all they point us to the one who is unshakable—Christ, our cornerstone.

So here are some of the things that were written in Psalms. Some are from authors aside from David; they too resonate. These words are some of the cries *for* help and some of the revelations *of* help. If you'd like a copy of these specific psalms to cut out and take with you—put somewhere special—you can find them at https://tinyurl.com/Psalms-for-the-Broken.

And remember, when the word speaks of the help God gives to the righteous—this is you! It is not based on anything you've done or are doing. It is not negated by the way you are feeling. It is the righteousness of Christ—imputed to you (2 Cor 5:21). If Jesus is your Savior, it is done already. It is yours simply because of the price he paid in shedding his blood. So receive it. You *do not* deserve it—that is the whole point of mercy. Your current mental illness does not make you *less* worthy, because you are *never* worthy at all, no matter how "well" you may be, at any stage of your life. *That* is the goodness of God—it is yours free, his gift to you (Eph 2:8). Now read the consequences. If you do not know Jesus as your Savior then all you have to do is ask him and believe. "If you confess with your mouth, 'Jesus is Lord,' and believe in your heart that God raised him from the dead, you will be saved. For it is with your heart that you believe and are justified, and it is with your mouth that you confess and are saved" (Rom 10:9–10). Find a good Bible-believing church so you can be encouraged and have peers and mentors to support you. This is also part of the provision of God for us in giving other people in our lives (1 Cor 12:27).

I also include some verses where David prays about relief from his enemies. This still applies so powerfully to us today as the apostle Paul has told us we wrestle not against flesh and blood but against the rulers, against the authorities, against the powers of this dark world and against the spiritual forces of evil in the heavenly realms (Eph 6:12). So pray these prayers because we surely do wrestle! Consider even the story of when Elisha opened his servant's eyes to see the vast army of God that outnumbered the enemy (2 Kgs 6:15–17). Hear those same words spoken for you today in your battle—"Those that are with us are more than those that are with them."

I pray you can both cry out *and* find that loving hand that God places on you (Ps 139:5). I pray that you will be able to read and meditate with open ears to hear the greatest counselor there is, the Holy Spirit living in you, speak and minister to you. Don't skip over the verses with some notion of familiarity. Take the time to reflect on thoughts and words that come to you as you read, that align with his word and his character. If something jumps out, runs deep, meditate on it, read it again, commit it to memory. When you feel you don't even have a prayer to pray, pray *these* words; even when you can pray, pray these as well. Reflect on his love for you. It is unending and unconditional. There is now no condemnation for those who are in Christ Jesus (Rom 8:1) If there is nothing you can do right now, if you cannot even muster strength to pray, then just read his words. Read about who *he* is. You are not alone in your struggles; David related, many others do too, and God is with you no matter what the outlook, the situation, the feeling, the weakness, the inability. His love, strength, and faithfulness are more real than what is in front of you right now—and you don't have to "feel" that way for it to be true. And God is for you; and if God is for you, then who can be against you (Rom 8:32)?

Answer me when I call to you, O my righteous God. Give me relief from my distress; be merciful to me and hear my prayer. (Ps 4:1)

I will lie down in peace and sleep; for you alone, O LORD, make me dwell in safety. (Ps 4:8)

I am worn out from groaning; all night long I flood my bed with weeping and drench my couch with tears. My eyes grow weak with sorrow; they fail because of all my foes. Away from me, all you who do evil, for the LORD has heard my weeping. The LORD has heard my cry for mercy; the LORD accepts my prayer. All my enemies will be ashamed and dismayed; they will turn back in sudden disgrace. (Ps 6:6–10)

The LORD is a refuge for the oppressed, a stronghold in times of trouble. Those who know your name will trust in you, for you, LORD, have never forsaken those who seek you. (Ps 9:9–10)

How long must I wrestle with my thoughts and day after day have sorrow in my heart? How long will my enemy triumph over me? . . . But I trust in your unfailing love; my heart rejoices in your salvation. I will sing the LORD's praise, for he has been good to me. (Ps 13:2, 5–6)

The LORD is my rock, my fortress and my deliverer; my God is my rock, in whom I take refuge, my shield and the horn of my salvation, my stronghold. I called to the LORD, who is worthy of praise, and I have been saved from my enemies. The cords of death coiled around me; the snares of death confronted me. In my distress I called to the LORD; I cried to my God for help. From his temple he heard my voice; my cry came before him, into his ears. . . . He rescued me from my powerful enemy, from my foes, who were too strong for me. (Ps 18:2–6, 17)

You, O LORD, keep my lamp burning; my God turns my darkness into light. (Ps 18:28)

(Read all of Ps 18—how angry God became that someone dare touch his beloved child, how he thundered with passion from heaven to come to David's rescue—and set

him in a spacious place because he delighted in his child
[v. 19].)

The LORD is my Shepherd,
I shall not be in want.
He makes me lie down in green pastures,
he leads me beside quiet waters,
he restores my soul.
He guides me in paths of righteousness for his name's sake.
Even though I walk through the valley of the shadow of death,
I will fear no evil, for you are with me;
Your rod and your staff, they comfort me.
You prepare a table before me
In the presence of my enemies.
You anoint my head with oil;
My cup overflows.
Surely goodness and love will follow me
All the days of my life,
And I will dwell in the house of the LORD forever. (Ps 23)

(Consider his leading, provision, protection, presence.)

To you, Oh LORD, I lift up my soul. (Ps 25:1)

All the ways of the LORD are loving and faithful.
(Ps 25:10a)

My eyes are ever on the LORD, for only he will release my
feet from the snare. Turn to me and be gracious to me,
for I am lonely and afflicted. The troubles of my heart
have multiplied; free me from my anguish. (Ps 25:15–17)

The LORD is my light and my salvation—whom shall I
fear? The LORD is the stronghold of my life—of whom
shall I be afraid? . . . For in the day of trouble he will keep
me safe in his dwelling; he will hide me in the shelter
of his sacred tent and set me high upon a rock. . . . Wait
for the LORD; be strong and take heart and wait for the
LORD. (Ps 27:1, 5, 14)

You turned my wailing into dancing; you removed my
sackcloth and clothed me with joy. (Ps 30:11)

Turn your ear to me, come quickly to my rescue; be my rock of refuge, a strong fortress to save me. . . . I will be glad and rejoice in your love, for you saw my affliction and knew the anguish of my soul. . . . Be merciful to me, LORD, for I am in distress; my eyes grow weak with sorrow, my soul and my body with grief. . . . But I trust in you, O LORD; I say, "You are my God." My times are in your hands; deliver me from the hands of my enemies, from those who pursue me. . . . Praise be to the LORD, for he showed me the wonders of his love when I was in a city under siege. (Ps 31:2, 7, 9, 14–15, 21)

You are my hiding place; you will protect me from trouble and surround me with songs of deliverance. (Ps 32:7)

The LORD is close to the brokenhearted and saves those who are crushed in spirit. (Ps 34:18)

I am bowed down and brought very low; all day long I go about mourning. . . . I am feeble and utterly crushed; I groan in anguish of heart. All my longings lie open before you, O LORD; my sighing is not hidden from you. My heart pounds, my strength fails me; even the light has gone from my eyes. . . . LORD, I wait for you; you will answer, Lord my God. . . . LORD, do not forsake me; do not be far from me, my God. Come quickly to help me, my Lord and my Savior. (Ps 38:6, 8–10, 15, 21–22)

Why are you downcast, O my soul? Why so disturbed within me? Put your hope in God, for I will yet praise him, my Savior and my God. (Ps 42:5)

Evening, morning and noon I cry out in distress, and he hears my voice. He ransoms me unharmed from the battle waged against me, even though many oppose me. (Ps 55:17–18)

Cast your cares on the LORD and he will sustain you; he will never let the righteous be shaken. (Ps 55:22)

From the ends of the earth I call to you, I call as my heart grows faint; lead me to the rock that is higher than I. For you have been my refuge, a strong tower against my foe. (Ps 61:2–3)

Save me, O God, for the waters have come up to my neck. I sink in the miry depths, where there is no foothold. I have come into the deep waters; the floods engulf me. I am worn out calling for help; my throat is parched. My eyes fail, looking for my God. . . . Do not let the flood-waters engulf me or the depths swallow me up or the pit close its mouth over me. Answer me, LORD, out of the goodness of your love; in your great mercy turn to me. (Ps 69:1–3, 15–16)

When anxiety was great within me, your consolation brought joy to my soul. (Ps 94:19)

Be at rest once more, O my soul, for the LORD has been good to you. (Ps 116:7)

My comfort in my suffering is this: Your promise preserves my life. (Ps 119:50)

Your word is a lamp for my feet, a light on my path. (Ps 119:105)

You know when I sit and when I rise; you perceive my thoughts from afar. You discern my going out and my lying down; you are familiar with all my ways. Before a word is on my tongue, you, LORD, know it completely. You hem me in behind and before, and you lay your hand upon me. . . . If I say, "Surely the darkness will hide me and the light become night around me," even the darkness will not be dark to you; the night will shine like the day, for darkness is as light to you. (Ps 139:2–5, 11–12)

When my spirit grows faint within me, it is you who knows my way. (Ps 142:3a)

I cry to you, O LORD; I say, "You are my refuge, my portion in the land of the living." Listen to my cry, for I am in desperate need; rescue me from those who pursue me, for they are too strong for me. Set me free from my prison, that I may praise your name. (Ps 142:5–7)

Answer me quickly, O LORD; my spirit fails. Do not hide your face from me or I will be like those who go down to the pit. Let the morning bring me word of your unfailing love, for I have put my trust in you. Show me the way I should go, for to you I lift up my soul. (Ps 143:7–8)

The LORD upholds all those who fall and lifts up all who are bowed down. (Ps 145:14)

6

In the Driver's Seat

MICHELLE STOPPED IN HER tracks. Her heart skipped a beat. Matt was hitching the van to the car. This was it. The kids were already crammed into the back seat, practically frothing at the mouth as they tore through preprepared puzzle books and homework folders, comparing notes like caffeinated academics.

They were ready to leave.

This was fine. This was not a big deal. This was nothing to worry about. It was exciting. She took a deep breath and moved another step forward towards the loaded-up car.

Three months in outback Australia was exciting. The ultimate plan of an extended trip had whispered to them through the years and now finally its voice was loud and present. The exhilaration was unmatched, but the dreaded companion that had come to haunt Michelle over the years would not be left behind.

Anxiety.

It was an enemy that had subtly worked its way into her inner circle. She had opened the door at times. Often unaware, she let it overstay—and it took full advantage, growing and claiming ownership of her body, thoughts and emotions. This trip was fertile ground for its eruption, with new experiences and unknowns around every corner.

She tried to focus on the truth of the positive despite the resident demon lurking. It meant no school, no strictness, no schedule. But it had taken months to prepare the house—agonizing months spent appointing near-strangers to care for the animals, second-guessing every decision, organizing details and tying up loose ends. Everything building up like a Jenga masterpiece of balance and positioning. One wrong move and the tower would come tumbling down.

Michelle smiled at the kids; oblivious, wild with anticipation, completely unaware of the negative narrative that looped relentlessly through her mind like a slow-working poison. This was the stuff nightmares were made of. This was teeth-clenching material and Michelle swore her hair was grayer for it.

Matt's hair was unchanged from the mouse brown that he'd always had. He came around from the back of the car and laid his hand on her shoulder. He knew the demons that hounded her. If all they did was change her hair color, she was lucky. "We're good to go. You all set?"

She exhaled slowly and nodded. "Good to go."

The road north was familiar at first. Michelle sat steeped in thoughts, sinking into the muddled depths of her mind. It would take a few hundred kilometers of travel before they were covering new ground. Michelle figured she'd need at least that long to get her thoughts under control. She hoped the paracetamol would bring her throbbing head and churning stomach into submission, but it could not offer her the buoyancy she needed to escape the drowning depths of the myriad of dark thoughts that plagued her.

Yes, the caravan was old but surely it was unlikely to fall apart. Surely everyone's health would stay intact, surely they wouldn't get abducted or murdered, surely they would not all perish in a ball of flames. She scoffed at herself and shook her head as she realized *normal* people didn't think like this. *Normal* people would not believe how much she let her thoughts run away. Give her five seconds and she could imagine the paramedics, the hospital staff, the trauma of notifying next of kin. She could see the headlines, feel the terror, tally the finances. It ticked on and on like a lit fuse, burning steadily toward detonation. Michelle started to breathe slowly and deeply, the only technique she had . . . that and prayer.

"God, please look after us. Thank you for this chance to see your amazing creation."

She let the gratitude that bubbled beneath the lava rise up and pop on the surface for the fraction of time it would take before the fire engulfed it afresh. "This is going to be such an adventure," she said as she turned her head slightly back to be in the kids' earshot. "All the new things we will see will be so exciting." The children looked up, smiled, and cast a momentary glance out the window before attempting to return to their activities, but it had been enough of a distraction and they closed their books in unison. They started some innocent jostling and soon enough Matt put on an audiobook of Roald Dahl's classics, and once again the voices in the car went silent as everyone took in some new scenery and listened to *The Twits*.

The first few nights of camping were enough to settle Michelle into a sense of adventure and intrigue, and the campfire songs and games were something that memories were made of. Still, the claws of anxiety lingered in the darkness, waiting for an opportunity to pounce and tear skin and expose bone.

Michelle's lifeline of prayer had brought her mind to reflect on Psalm 23, and over and over in her head as each new road was traveled "Goodness and mercy . . . Goodness and mercy" was playing on repeat like a sacred rhythm. Each repetition pushed back the fear, inch by inch. Anxiety retreated to a reasonable distance, waiting to strike as all the while, Michelle's faith grew as she whispered the words of truth into the silence. "Surely goodness and mercy will follow me all the days of my life."

The second week of the trip, they hit the Oodnadatta Track in searing desert heat. Michelle had leaned across to Matt's side to snap a picture of the "40° C" read out mocking them from the dash. The kids, oblivious to the rising temperature, merrily improvised on ukulele and were soon singing a song they'd uniquely titled "Oodnadatta Track." But as the knowledge of the solitude, the heat, and the distance struck home, Michelle began to breathe heavily as all the worst-case scenarios began circling her mind like vultures scenting fresh meat.

"*Family lost in the desert,*"

"*Father suffers heatstroke leaving family stranded,*"

"*Car breaks down in wilderness forcing an early end to trip of a lifetime.*"

The counterfeit headlines blared across her mind's front page and when the loud crunch did come, she stopped breathing completely, poised for the impending drama.

Everyone was sweating, the air con a luxury that was used sparingly in extreme heat to save the motor, and now they were stuck. Matt was soon busy crawling around under the van in the oppressive heat only to discover the caravan suspension had completely torn in two.

"Goodness and mercy, goodness and mercy . . . "

Everyone found a spot in the only shade available next to the van and the lemonade was brought out of the fridge and shared around as Matt examined, diagnosed, and began work on a solution. The kids ran around in the searing sand, exploring, unconcerned about the heat or isolation. "Watch out for snakes" was Matts only instruction but it caused a million more disasters to present themselves to Michelle's imagination, and she watched on with shallow breath as a hollow ache pounded behind her ribs.

No snakes were seen that sweltering afternoon and within a few hours Matt had worked his magic—wire coiled tight around the chassis, holding the wounded van together just enough to limp toward the nearest populated campsite. The immediate threat was neutralized.

Michelle's mind, however, refused to move on, working overtime, looping and digging deep, reaching for hell. Yet somehow, that same psalm kept surfacing, like driftwood rising through murky tide, bringing her back, drawing her attention. "Thy rod and thy staff. My cup overflows. Goodness and mercy."

They made it off the outback track and reached Coward Springs, where a natural hot spring steamed beside relics of an older world—century-old telegraph wire now able to be repurposed to brace the van further for the thousand-kilometer stretch ahead that would get them to Alice Springs where some professional help would be available.

The thought of the wire rattling loosely under the van forced Michelle into a tight bundle of stress as they drove on. Her prayers lifted heavenward as her teeth clenched with every bounce. Deep breathing and prayer . . . deep breathing and prayer. Hold it together . . . hold it together.

It was a long stretch, but the welding job in Alice was successful and gave the van new strength, and Michelle a rest from tight muscles and wearied mind. They were ready for the notorious ruts of the Tanami Track.

From there, something shifted. With each passing day, they shed tension like dust from their shoulders. They were beginning to breathe again—laughing more, marveling, moving with a kind of lightness. Matt still had to screw cabinets back in or patch up some new break each evening, but the old van held together. Michelle, now cresting the roller coaster of fear, gazed out at the wide-open land, drinking in its majesty, all the while playing on repeat, "Goodness and mercy . . . Goodness and mercy . . ."

There were still incidents, of course. There always would be. They did not manage to unravel Michelle at this point, though they cried out for her attention like toll bells in a high-vaulted cathedral; the heat exhaustion at Wolfe Creek, infestations of bugs at the edge of the Tanami, eerie rustlings in the scrub at night and dingoes howling across a moonless sky.

Each called Michelle to worry, to tension, to stress, but their call was distant. The fear didn't grip the same way. The unknown no longer whispered only threat—it whispered adventure.

Goodness and mercy. Mercy and goodness.

She began to revel in it—the wide skies, the red dust, the distances that declared God's glory. Found in a spacious place, in the middle of nowhere with only a slight sense of trepidation that was mingled with awe and excitement.

Michelle rejoiced in the new scenery and experiences, and Matt's ability to improvise, repair, and provide became more than a skill set—it was divine provision. Every solution felt like a whisper of God's goodness, a quiet answer to the prayers she hadn't even known how to form.

This *was* a trip of a lifetime, and slowly, she was beginning to see it. The noises and stresses at home were food for the demon that hounded. Here, he was being starved. Here, there was space, and time, and quiet and distance, and everything was declaring Gods glory.

The high had carried her further than she realized. In her thankfulness and relief, she'd loosened her grip—just enough for the enemy to slip through. She'd forgotten how subtly he worked, how even joy could be twisted if her guard fell. He crept in quietly, needling at the edges of gratitude. The descent was near.

"Thank you for our trip," Michelle prayed continuously as they settled into the dust, heat, and isolation of Northern Australia. "Thank you for this opportunity, our safety, our health. Thank you for your beauty. I know I need to give my anxieties to you. I know you can take them all. Thank you for this restoration, the green pastures and still waters . . . "

She paused mid-prayer.

Out of nowhere, that ever-lurking enemy seized on the last two words and drove them deep into her conscience like blades. They lodged in her mind like splinters—small but impossibly sharp—pressing deeper with each breath, twisting meaning into a storm of irrational fear and spiraling "what-ifs."

Michelle had fought for so long to focus on God's goodness, to cling to the truth despite the mounting uncertainties: her own faltering resolve, the unforgiving outback terrain, the isolation, the terrifying lack of control.

The Jenga tower toppled.

Her resolve gave way, crumbling like an avalanche. Anxieties echoed in the vast silence, and the still waters of her prayer turned turbulent. Her soul recoiled.

Even knowing her Lord's omniscience, she felt a desperate urge to speak, to *tell* him—as if he might not see the dread beneath the surface unless she named it. "Lord," she cried, "you know what lurks beneath those still waters! You realize we're now in saltwater crocodile country?"

The little knowledge she had of this giant, killer reptile exploded beyond the realm of fact. Images tore through her mind—headlines, grave-faced anchors, distraught families, sympathetic strangers.

"Australia's primordial relic reigns as one of nature's most efficient predators, hidden beneath still, lily-padded waters or lurking in mud near the shore. Unaware tourists venture too close to the edge, never knowing the beast lies in wait for unsuspecting children to be his next meal. With jaws that snap shut like a steel trap and crush bone in an instant, he drags his victims beneath the surface and performs a violent death roll until drowning ensues . . ."

Michelle shook her head as the images cascaded in nonstop repetition in her mind's eye. A child slipping, a scream cut short, the sickening silence of swallowed air. Her own voice, begging. Her feet, frozen.

It was more than her anxious heart could bear. The background whisper trying to warn her of her unrealistic catastrophizing had never been strong enough to tip the scales. The trip of a lifetime plummeted once more into the depths of a thousand dark imaginings. The calm was gone—the ancient gorges and cascading waterfalls, the pristine water holes, the thrill of trekking stony paths, the promise of goodness and mercy—all pushed out of reach.

Those wonder-filled experiences now seemed like distant echoes, drowned beneath the rising tide of panic. They had been fueling her—buoying courage and joy, filling her with gratitude—but none of it mattered now. Those things became irrelevant in the wake of what this danger could entail. It all collapsed under the imagined weight of crushing crocodile jaws.

Would I dive in after them if a croc took them? Do I poke it in the eyes? How long will the pain last in the thrashing of the death roll until drowning? Matt would surely jump in; I would lose them all. Do I need to know where the nearest hospital is? Where is the closest phone reception?

A brief whisper of "goodness and mercy" flickered across her thoughts like wind across water—but it was no match for the roar of imagined splashes and horror of the death roll. Even her body betrayed her as her stomach responded to the lit fuse and twisted into sickening cramps and tightness. She welcomed the pain in place of the crushing crocodile bite she feared awaited.

Matt saw the change in his wife the first time the kids plunged into the first water hole available. He'd done the research—signs were posted, and locals and rangers were always ready to advise if something was croc-free—but even a wet big toe was causing Michelle to panic. He tried to reassure her, and when they weren't sure, they didn't let the kids anywhere near the water, but the beast had awoken and the claws were already well and truly embedded.

Croc country was going to consume a large portion of their trip and Michelle knew she would either have to deal with it or give up all together. Would she seriously pull Matt and the children away from such an adventure and insist they head home? How could she do that to them? How would they react to her? What if none of them spoke to her anymore? What if she was cut off and disappeared behind her own silence . . .

At least they'd be alive.

Michelle shook her head as she realized her thoughts were spiraling.

Matt pulled them up in a solitary camp spot on the Gregory River. They'd spent the day exploring a fossil site and Michelle tried to keep her thoughts occupied with the safe and true. "Goodness and mercy, goodness and mercy . . ." It was still only a faint whisper against the fears, but Michelle grasped intentionally at it with all the strength she could muster. If this was what it meant to take thoughts captive, she was using the strongest of bonds, but her tying-up techniques needed some work.

They were camped a good 250 meters away from the river and that was declared safe from crocs; in fact, Matt tried to reassure, they were probably too far inland for crocs now anyway. Michelle didn't underestimate the voracious predator. Hiding unsuspectingly was his forté, like her anxious thoughts that consumed suddenly when all had seemed safe. She tried her best to ignore the anxiety and join in with the family. The standard practice of campfire games and campsite exploration was underway, but as they examined the river and the narrow, concrete causeway the fast waters were surging over, Matt exclaimed the obvious—tomorrow they would need to cross.

River crossings hadn't troubled Michelle much until now. Matt knew what he was doing and the waters hadn't been too deep. This was different. Anxiety was at its height and needed no pushing to go over the edge. This causeway was barely wide enough for the vehicle and the water gushed across it with a force capable of sweeping anything—or anyone—into oblivion. A friendly ranger happened by as they stood assessing the crossing and, to Michelle's dismay, nonchalantly declared, "Oh yes, cars do go over the edge of the causeway all the time!"

The words detonated in Michelle's mind. Her anxiety surged like the torrent before her, her thoughts spiraling at breakneck speed, leaving her breathless and unmoored. She could not concentrate on anything after that. Her head was reeling, her stomach was responding with its usual churning, and she could not even eat. "Oh God help!" she prayed in continued desperation as the evening approached. The beautiful, outback pastel dusk went unnoticed as the blackened depths of doom consumed. "Please get us across safely, please help. I know that you are good no matter what happens." But her prayers did not bring sleep, and she found that as she tossed and turned and fidgeted through the night, all she could do was keep praying for help to come in the morning.

They were a long way from civilization. What would happen if they did go over the causeway, were there salties in there? Even if they were safe from those monsters, what would be the next step, with a car and caravan sideways in a turbulent river? Michelle realized her thoughts were sideways in a turbulent river, and she was about to drown.

Michelle was oblivious to the morning pack-up. Everything was happening on autopilot as the claws continued to tear at her. All of the "what-ifs" and "what-thens" were shouting down any whisper of "goodness and mercy," and her throbbing head made it almost impossible to get anything done. Matt carried the weight as usual and tried to keep upbeat, but Michelle could not miss that even he was wary as he told the kids to leave their seat belts off and windows open, preparing for worst-case scenario.

Somehow, she found a shallow spot upstream where she managed to cross to the other side in relative safety without the terror of hidden predators or fear of being knocked down in the fierce flow that buffeted the causeway. She made her way back to the road and waited on the other side, camera in hand, pretending that she was not just about to go into heart failure. "Oh God please, oh God please . . ." She tried to reassure herself that even if they went over, this was but a hiccup in life; so many people were experiencing worse every day, but it did not make her anxiety lessen and it did not ease the excruciating tearing and biting that made it hard to breathe. She tried to stop clenching her teeth, knowing it might ease the headache, but it was all involuntary. The enemy had taken hold. "God, I know you are good, no matter what . . ." But despite her declaration, her hidden fears were a key for doubt. It unlocked her battered soul's door and entered ruthlessly. "Do I believe that?" Her heart faltered and she shook her head. "I mustn't believe that, when my body reacts this way. I'm so sorry God." Now this train of thought took over and her pure panic set in as she despaired that even her faith was false. "If my Spirit is stronger than my body, then I wouldn't be experiencing all these physical sensations. If I believed, it would overcome my body's reaction." She swallowed hard to try to subdue the nausea and one by one rubbed her sweaty palms on her khaki shorts. Time had slowed, and as a breeze of fresh air brushed past Michelle's tense face in a graceful motion of the unexpected hand of God, her dwindling faith awakened, and Michelle grasped at the small shield in desperation to extinguish the fiery darts of the enemy. "Oh God! I do. Yes—I do! I do believe! I have tasted and seen. I know you are good no matter what. No matter what happens now, no matter how my body responds to my worries, you are still stronger and greater. I know you help through every circumstance we face and are with us. Oh God, how do I pass that deep truth on to my body, on to my mind? How do I make my flesh align with my spirit? Teach me your ways. Get me across to the other side . . . please . . . get us across to the other side."

Michelle hit "record" on the camera with shaky fingers as the nose of the vehicle rounded the corner at the top of the hill and Matt descended into the nightmare. He drove slowly and cautiously, lining everything up, but as the full length of the van hit the water, Michelle's prayers turned into a guttural plea of desperation as she watched the caravan wheel slip off the causeway. "Oh *God*! Oh *God*!" Matt and the kids were oblivious it had even gone over, as it only took a second for Matt's true steering to drag the van back onto the causeway and in a moment they were pulling up next to Michelle with water cascading all around the sides of the van. Matt got out to inspect the aftermath and jovially circled the vehicles. Michelle's hand was at her chest as she tried to stop hyperventilating. "The wheel went over!" She was rasping, and Matt had raised his eyebrows, pursed his lips, and nodded as he considered the implications, but nothing more was said, only that reassuring hand on her shoulder, as was his way.

Michelle stood recovering—but only just. Her heart was no longer pounding in her ears, but the ache in her chest still lingered like an echo. The fog in her head was beginning to clear, yet her stress had weighed her down so much she was exhausted. Her muscles ached. Every part of her had been tensed for so long, she didn't know how to release it. Every breath was a decision.

Matt, by contrast, was energized. He thrived on the unpredictability of the outback, fully present, guiding the car through the rough terrain with an ease born of quiet confidence. He didn't ignore the danger, he just dealt with it, did not let it consume, moved on. The kids continued on in their oblivion; naïve, innocent, beautifully untouched by the storm their mother had just weathered. One of them leaned halfway out the window, dusty cheeks flushed from sun, and shouted cheerfully, "What's for lunch?" The absurdity of the question nearly made Michelle laugh—almost. Her lips twitched. A moment ago she had been bracing for death, and now they were requesting sandwiches. She almost collapsed to the ground. Did they not know they could have drowned? They could have been something else's lunch! They could have had their lives washed away! They hadn't seen the battle inside her, and that was indeed a mercy. Proof that not everything broke, just because she did.

She got back into the passenger seat next to Matt as though she were retreating from battle, shaky, spent and rubbing her fingers on her pounding head as he drove on.

"Thank you God," Michelle whispered from her depths. She turned back to the kids and shook her head. What was going on in their brains?

Something was stirring in her spirit as the whispers of goodness and mercy tried to regain her attention. She glanced at the children a second time. Why were they so free from anxiety, why were they not even marginally . . . normally concerned?

Matt interrupted her thoughts as he spoke loudly to them all, "Look at that landscape!" They all looked out as the low bush thinned and a vast desert expanse spread before them. Spinifex dotted the sandy roadside and a small group of red goshawks soared up ahead. The blazing midday sun injected brightness and beauty into everything it touched, and the golden glow dripped thick like honey. Michelle looked over at Matt and nodded. She suddenly realized the answer to the mystery.

She turned back to the kids, who were looking at the beauty too—the same beauty that had surrounded them ten minutes ago, yesterday, last year. Beauty that had never left. Beauty despite the darkness, in fact, all through it. Beauty that declared an omnipotent creator God and loving Father whose word said he laid it all out for their pleasure. The kids sat with smiles and random chatter to each other. The back seat was clear. There was no tormenting monster there, nothing clawing at them, nothing to squash their joy or steal their excitement.

Michelle turned back to the road. The red, sandy, sunburnt country, rocky outcrops, glowing flora, gently pulled her back to the present, grounding her in its steady embrace. "Goodness and mercy" began to echo powerfully within her spirit, louder now than the lies and filling her with a sense of peace and renewal.

She turned to face her husband again as she considered how he drew their attention to the surrounding beauty whilst navigating the current sand and ruts. The children had looked, as he had directed them, and their eyes glowed with fascination and intrigue. Their truth was deepening inside her as she contemplated what had been happening this whole trip. The truth that could set free, the secret revealed . . .

They trusted the driver.

They knew *he* knew where he was going and how to get there. They knew, even in their limited capacity, that he knew how to drive—that he was the best one to be at the wheel. They knew there was no cause for worry as long as their dad was driving. He was in control and they could just sit back and enjoy the ride. Sure, there'd be danger at times, sure, there were pot holes and ruts, but he'd give them instructions when needed. He'd tell them to hold on and he'd bring them through.

Michelle turned her eyes towards *her* driver as she glanced in awe at the wide open expanse of outback Australia and the vaulted, vast, clear blue sky above. *Her* driver steered true and straight and pulled her careening carriage back onto the track, and as she acknowledged who was at the wheel, anxiety stuck its tail between its legs, curled over in defeat, and fled in humiliated terror.

Michelle began to hum the hymn she had learned as a child as the words of truth swirled in her head and rooted deeply into her heart.

The Lord's my Shepherd, I'll not want;
  He makes me down to lie
In pastures green; He leadeth me
  The quiet waters by.
My soul He doth restore again,
  And me to walk doth make
Within the paths of righteousness,
  E'en for His own name's sake.

Yea, though I walk in death's dark vale,
　Yet will I fear none ill;
For Thou art with me, and Thy rod
　And staff me comfort still.

My table Thou hast furnished
　In presence of my foes;
My head Thou dost with oil anoint,
　And my cup overflows.

Goodness and mercy all my life
　Shall surely follow me,
And in God's house forevermore
　My dwelling-place shall be.

The Lord is my Shepherd . . . I lack nothing . . . He leads me beside still waters . . . He restores my soul . . . I will fear no evil for your rod and staff comfort me . . . He prepares for me in the presence of my enemies . . . My cup overflows.

Michelle's cup was overflowing. The repetition in her mind just served to release more freedom, and in it she reveled. She was establishing a new understanding. New thoughts were swirling. Things happen to people all the time; sometimes good, sometimes bad, sometimes big, sometimes small. It is the nature of life. It is inevitable. Overwhelming, difficult, or even events of unexpected rejoicing can happen in the blink of an eye to anyone. Change is constant and challenging, but the Lord is the same yesterday, today, and forever. Unchanging, faithful, true, and loving, and these things are certain.

Matt patted Michelle's knee in excitement. "I'm loving this road," he said happily, and Michelle giggled as her thoughts continued to strengthen and tear down strongholds.

"If the Lord is my Shepherd, then he is out in front and leads me through it all. There is nothing else I have need of and surely goodness and mercy will follow me all the days of my life."

Michelle sighed, this time in peace. She knew she did not have the answers about anxiety and how it worked, the propensity for some people to struggle, the help and strategies that were available, the self-condemnation that added to the struggle, but she smiled as she recognized something that she had known all along. That God knows. That he did not condemn, that he was the driver, the good Shepherd, the rock.

Michelle looked over at Matt again and placed her hand on his knee as they smiled at each other.

What a gift it was to embark on this journey—navigating sandy tracks, swimming in timeless canyons, leaping from cool waterfalls in the tropical heat, and falling asleep beneath a canopy of stars, free from the constraints of a schedule. All of this was incredible, but as he was prone to do, God had blessed exceedingly abundantly beyond what she could ask or imagine. He constantly revealed his beauty and glory in creation, but it was one glance at her children that had put her enemy to flight as she saw what trust looked like with childlike faith.

"My dad is taking me, leading me, over hill and through valley."

"My dad knows the tracks, the obstacles, the secret treasures along the way."

"My dad knows how to steer and tells me when to look and when to hold on. He gives me everything I need."

There was still a long way to go on this trip but now Michelle's thoughts turned homeward. She would need to allow God to steer her through the known pitfalls at home, to be the one to navigate the trigger paths and obstacles.

Michelle continued to smile and spoke a quiet word to her enemy. "Oh anxiety. I know sometimes I let you come in. I open the door and hand you the keys, let you take the reins. I know sometimes you trip me with one little trigger when my guard is down. But you don't have any authority. You're not the winner. You don't have any right, and you are not as strong as my true lead and Lord and master. He's overcome you."

"And you know what?" Michelle continued out loud, and Matt looked over in curiosity at her sudden question. She glanced sideways at him and smiled.

"Jesus is the best driver . . . and goodness and mercy are following right behind . . .

All the days of my life."

7

Fear vs. Faith

"This is the victory that has overcome the world, even our faith."

1 JOHN 5:4

Is there magic; thunder; wonder, within a mustard seed
Or power profound external?
Will mountain be moved by fingers of faith,
Or mighty hand eternal?
Are occurrences of each day bound and set
Or answers to prayer to be found?
If creation declares your glory and name
Why does deafness abound?

Do I lack faith if I'm blind to your activity?

If free will . . . my choices, determine quality of life
How does your sovereignty reign?
If my heart fades and soul shrinks at the weight of my failure
How do I stand up again?
If it all stems from faith, where are you in that?
It's just shadow of positive thought

Or does hope lie only in omnipotence, omniscience,
Love unconditional, undeserved and unsought?

Is the strength to choose faith over fear yours or mine?

Your still, small voice whispers. Your presence, gentle.
The enemy's subtle lies deafen.
In the depths of the pit do I struggle to climb
Or will you reach down and lift me to heaven?
Is your binding of brokenness so hard to reach
When hurt blasts a hole in my heart,
When internal questions rock the foundations
Am I left shaking back at the start?

Is the fear that what you say is not true?

My faith weak like cotton, fear strong like steel,
Is this tug of war fair?
Disqualification looms heavy like chains,
Your freedoms like mist in the air.
If your word is alive and cuts like a sword,
Dividing my flesh and my soul,
How do I surrender to slashing and pain
And let you be the one in control?

Is surrender the antidote to fear?

If reconciliation by you has been won,
Why can't I settle the truth?
The unending war between earthly—eternal,
To have faith like an innocent youth.
The truth is in knowing you're more real than "this,"
For now we see only in part,
Greater than all I can think, feel, or see,
Faith extinguishing the foe's fiery dart.

Who will I choose to believe?

To each has been given a portion of faith,
Mine, maybe, is small like that seed

Yet if world's overcome and righteousness credited
Perhaps that is all that I need.
Faith can't make you bigger or stronger or more
(Nor fear make you weaker and small);
You are, after all, the only "I AM,"
King of Kings and Lord over all!

You are God alone, despite my measure of faith.

If you're all that you say, and I know that you are,
Why are doubt and fear so strong?
If I'm stumbling and struggling to be who I should
That's not evidence the whole tenet's wrong.
I know there are miracles at one word from your mouth;
Why does it seem you stand far?
A plethora of forever unraveling questions,
I *will* simply believe who you are.

Faith is the assurance of things hoped for.
Perfect love drives out fear.

8

A Brighter Light

I HAD TO GET out. The walls of the house were closing in, the air turning suffocating as if it conspired to crush me. Staying wasn't an option; the torment was clawing at my chest, and I knew it wouldn't leave me, not really. The enemy was inside—impossible to outrun, but I had to try. The familiarity of everything around me screamed my incompetence and weakness.

Though the dark country roads around me beckoned, they did not comfort—they accused, but if I could just drive into the rainy night and see if there was somewhere beyond, somewhere I could stay afloat . . .

Distance called as though it could offer relief. I knew it could not. My chest heaved as the weight of my own thoughts threatened to pull me under. I stumbled into the car, fingers trembling as I gripped the wheel. I forced myself to turn the key, summoning every ounce of strength just to pull out of the driveway. No sudden movements, no screeching tires, just the slow, steady pace of someone who still looked in control, even as everything inside me cracked.

Left towards the country or right towards town? The question barely registered through the haze, but instinct pushed me left and instantly I felt the relief to be on the narrow country road, dark and empty. City traffic and blaring lights would have caused my already critical anxiety to flatline. The vents whirred to life, spilling cool air over my tear-streaked face as I drove blindly into the night. No plan, no destination. Just drive, and breathe, and hope the motion could keep me from falling apart completely.

My high beam illuminated the persistent drizzle, but the subtle scent that blew through those vents from the intermingled rain and surrounding bush was refreshing. I let my head fall back onto the headrest as I kept my eyes on the road and gritted my teeth as the guilt wracked my brain. What a loser I was that I could let my mind be so ravaged, and realistically there was absolutely no reason for it. The tears started afresh. Why could I not cope? What was I not coping with? I was ridiculous; a child standing on the seashore panicking at the ripples at my feet when others remained calm in the midst of their crashing waves and truly raging storms. What was this thing like a shadow that tormented me at every turn? Everything was overwhelming. What direction could I go? What decision could I make? Was there a way forward? I was drowning in the shallows.

The night pressed in around me as I drove down the narrow road, its darkness a silent companion. The rain clung to the drooping eucalypt leaves, catching the faint glow of my headlights and glistening like scattered diamonds. For a fleeting moment, I was drawn to the beauty of it, but the thought dissolved as quickly as it came, swallowed by the shadows. My mind wandered to the towering gums lining the road—magnificent sentinels that could end everything on impact. I shook the thought loose, unwilling to let it take root. Not tonight. Tonight I would drive, escape for a while, let myself breathe, let the tears fall. Then turn around, go home, slip into the pretense that everything was fine. Another pointless trip, another futile gesture—just like the rest of my life. Running from the emptiness, yet carrying the darkness within me wherever I went.

The intermittent drone of the wipers lulled me into a comatose autopilot and I was glad the road was a long one to nowhere in particular.

Suddenly my headlights blinked and I sat up to attention. The surrounding darkness had screamed the power of its presence for a split second and my adrenaline fired briefly with the fear of it. Instantly, that fear reared up and took control as the headlights fluttered off again . . . and stayed off. I slammed on the brakes and tried to keep the car straight. Everything was dark. I punched the hazard lights on and in their momentary blinks I could see I had veered and pulled up pointing directly at one of those beckoning gums. Ironic.

I turned the dial back and forth, but the lights were dead. I turned the engine off and on again—still nothing. I got out, not even trying to shelter from the dismal weather. I tried tapping forcefully on each of the headlights; still nothing.

I sank back into my driver's seat, wiping my damp face with a tired hand. My drizzle-soaked clothes clung to me, but I didn't care. It fit my mood perfectly—sunshine and happiness felt like distant strangers. Sitting here in the cold, damp darkness felt like exactly what I deserved. All I could do now was wait until a passerby happened along, and if that didn't happen, I guess it'd be about seven hours 'til daylight. At least my thoughts had been distracted momentarily, but now, as I sat with the hazards blinking, everything came flooding back and I began to think again of the situation I found myself in. Totally in the dark in more ways than one. I knew my condition. I knew the fiery darts that constantly shot at me. But it wasn't enough to cognitively assent that I was suffering from an illness. The acknowledgment didn't remove the hole. It didn't make it all go away. I needed more. I needed to know how to go forward, literally. My thoughts turned back to the fact that I was sitting stranded in the middle of the road. I wondered if I could drive with the blinkers on. Now there was a thought to dig deeper into that even brought a smirk to my face; driving with the blinkers on. Not a particularly clear way ahead, but maybe a way to move at least.

I was peering through the rain-soaked windscreen when I noticed a light approaching. It was blindingly bright, so intense I couldn't look directly at it. As it got closer, it went out and I could see much dimmer headlights and recognized the shape of a man on a four-wheeler motorbike. His shape was dark in the night, hooded in his soaking rain gear, but as he slowed and pulled alongside my driver's window, which I put down to greet him, I could see it was a rugged-looking bearded man—seemed a similar age to me. I'd never seen him around before. The flicker of kindness in his eyes was unmistakable but I was too detached to care. He could have been a serial killer and it wouldn't have mattered. Whatever was coming to me at this point might prove to be an escape from my unlit abyss.

"I saw your hazards flashing from my paddock up ahead. You OK?"

We introduced ourselves. He was Josh "from the farm down the road." I thanked him for coming and told him what had happened and popped the bonnet on his request. He checked things over for me, fiddled with the wiring, but nothing was working.

"Come up to the farmhouse," he offered. "My folks will get you a cuppa and we can sort it out. It's a fair way up the road and down a long driveway. Follow my light."

I nodded and he pulled in front and switched on his big floodlight which was mounted high on a pole on the back of his bike. I gasped in the shock of the contrast to the darkness I had been sitting in. The light stretched far ahead, spilling across the road and illuminating the trees on either side, as if daylight had suddenly broken through the night. I thought of my own feeble headlights and scoffed; even on high beam, they had never come close to revealing the path with such clarity. I switched on the motor and followed behind him.

We didn't go too fast and the drive was easy with everything so clearly seen around me. I followed comfortably, in quiet gratitude for my kind guide. We hadn't traveled far when I noticed that my headlights had flickered back to life. I beeped at Josh and he switched his powerful beam off and spun his bike around to greet me at my window again.

"My lights seem to be working now, I'll be fine to head on by myself."

He turned and looked at the road before us. "Mmm, they don't seem too bright to me."

I nodded knowingly. "Well no, not in contrast to yours! You're used to that light you have showing you everything!" Inwardly, I grimaced that our banter had brought a smile to my face. I wondered how genuine it looked parading over a tear-stained face as Josh continued.

"Seeing the road ahead is pretty important," he laughed. "I need to know where I'm going and what's around me when I'm out in the miserable darkness like this so often."

I nodded but didn't speak what I thought. "I'm out in the miserable darkness a lot too."

Josh went on, oblivious. "Well you go on ahead, I'll go behind for a while, gotta get to my turnoff anyway. I can make sure you'll be OK."

"Thank you so much."

I drove on and could see Josh traveling behind me with just his bike headlights on. After experiencing such an incredible light, it felt unsettling to navigate with only the faintest glow ahead. I had always been accustomed to this dimness, unaware there was something brighter, something better to guide me. Not far down the road, my headlights went out again. This time, I braked gently. I wasn't left completely in the dark, and the loss didn't feel as jarring as before. By the time Josh pulled up beside my window, the headlights flickered back on, offering their vague illumination of the way once more.

"I tend to think your lights mightn't be too trustworthy. Maybe we should just get you to the farmhouse and have a better look at things. I'll go back behind you, and you carry on for another 'K' or so. I'll pull back in front when we need to turn. I'll show you the way."

I sighed and nodded. "Sounds like a plan. Thanks again."

We headed off again with Josh behind me. This time he'd turned his floodlight back on and in the huge illumination, I could barely tell my lights were on at all. Occasionally as we drove along, I could see they flickered off, and then had come back on. On again and off again, but it did not make a difference to my way ahead as the light I was traveling by was so bright. My own light was swallowed by the brilliance that outshone it. I wondered how I would ever be able to go back to my dim things that were supposed to guide my way.

It wasn't long before he pulled back around beside me. The rain had eased and I was glad as he pulled up to my window to not have it misting my face as we spoke.

"There's a tree down ahead," he told me as I gazed forward. I nodded—I'd already noticed it in the clear glow of his light. It struck me that it would have crept up suddenly on me in this dark night if I had been driving by my own lights. "We can get around it, and the turnoff is just after that. Stick close to me. The recent rains have washed the road out a bit and it can be a bit tricky to navigate . . . another reason to follow this bright light."

Mmm, tricky to navigate. Like life. What was I doing here in the first place? This was my road wasn't it? Dark, dangerous, alone. I looked into Josh's eyes and nodded. Thankfully, unexpectedly, not alone. Someone to show me the way. Not just that, to take me with them; go behind and before, and light up the way with a constant and reliable light, not like my own.

Josh pulled out in front and I followed him closely forward, around the tree and up his driveway. We pulled up in front of an old farmhouse. The porch light was on. An older man in a flannel shirt stood in the doorway. Josh waited for me before heading in. "Calving's going fine, Dad," he said. "I'll check again in the morning. There's a tree down on the road; we might want to head down now and get the way cleared." Josh introduced me and explained my story. His father shook my hand and gestured for me to come inside.

"Merle's got the kettle on, love; I'll grab the chainsaw and we'll sort this tree out, Josh." He led me to their quaint kitchen where I met Josh's mum, Merle. She was in her dressing gown at the table with the kettle boiling on a slow combustion stove, waiting for her son's late-night return. The men headed off again and I sat with Merle as she placed a cup of tea in front of me. The table was laid with a checkered tablecloth and had a sugar bowl, salt and pepper shaker and an open Bible. I peered into my steaming cup. Merle exuded a warmth that made me comfortable, but I didn't know how to hide what had been happening for me in the last few hours as I had fallen into such a hole. I didn't know if I could cope being forced into company like this. My solitary hole beckoned and my very existence screamed my farce.

"Thanks for this," I said as I sipped.

"You're welcome dear," she said and placed her hand on mine. "I don't mind if you come by anytime if you need to talk or have a cuppa or anything."

I suppose my red eyes were a dead giveaway, but I wasn't so sure I was ready to open up to this stranger, lovely though she was. I thought I would just be general.

"It's been a rough day . . . a long one now. You guys are up late."

She nodded. "It's calving season. Josh has come home to help. He was just checking the heifers. So your headlights just stopped working?"

Again a nod. "Can't get far without them."

Merle pushed the open Bible towards me. "I was just reading about that," she placed a finger on a highlighted verse.

I read to myself. "'Your word is a lamp to guide me and a light to my path.'" I looked into her warm eyes and neither of us said anything for a short time. The turmoil inside me still raged. It had only been an hour ago I was questioning my lack of guidance and direction. "'Your word?'" I finally questioned.

She patted the Bible with affection. "God's word. It's a light. It's a map. It shows you the way. You've seen tonight what it's like to not have a light—to not be able to see your way. This is having the ultimate guide. The one who knows. The one who is."

I shook my head; she may have been talking about me not seeing without my headlights, but I didn't doubt she knew that her words went way deeper. "How is it a map?"

"He always knows the way, my love, no matter where you are. His word is alive and active. It is not dead. It is not passive. It will not return empty but will achieve that for which he sends it. He will use it however he pleases. It will show you the way." Her words were a little foreign to me but I felt like an ember flickered inside and I longed to fan the flame. Something somewhere was speaking to me. My breathing shallowed. It was like I was standing on the edge of a precipice and I needed to jump off. Into the unknown. Something beckoned.

She let her words rest for a moment as I contemplated. Was she saying this was the answer?

"How would I use it?" I couldn't comprehend the practicality of what she was saying.

Merle closed the Bible and pushed it even closer towards me. "You take this, dear. I have others and you can visit me anytime you like. You can open it, read, and have something burn in your soul. Or you will read, go away, and he will bring it to your attention when you need it in the future. It has the power to demolish strongholds, and it reveals his character. The more we learn we can trust him, how faithful and good he is, the more we can continue in joy on the journey we are on, no matter what comes our way."

I placed both hands on the book's cover, acknowledging her gift, but suddenly I felt ashamed, like I was hiding what was really going on and sitting before a new friend with a mask on. She'd mentioned the word "joy" as if it was something tangible. It was not something I could relate to. The tears came unwillingly. "I'm a mess. You don't know how I struggle. It's useless. . . . I'm useless. I'm sorry." I dropped my head onto my outstretched arms and lay there on the table feeling suddenly exhausted. I did not know how to muster the courage to jump off that precipice however strongly it summoned.

Merle's hands were immediately on mine. She drew her chair closer and put an arm over my shoulders. "Did you know that a hundred years ago, scientists listed over 180 body parts that they said were useless—had no function? Thankfully with advancements in technology and understanding, they are continually finding out that they were wrong in this regard."

I sat up, drank some more tea, and looked into her face as she went on.

"Those body parts continued to carry on doing their job, even when the experts didn't know what that was. Even when the experts thought they could be removed with no ill effect." She sighed, still smiling. "My point is that even if something appears useless, doesn't mean it is." She paused for a moment and I waited. "Even when the thing itself doesn't know its purpose, it continues to work, to be useful, in ways it couldn't even imagine." Her eyes went to the Bible. "This book tells me that you have been fearfully and wonderfully made. That means carefully, with precision, with purpose. That God knit you together in your mother's womb. I'm sorry I don't know what you have been through, what you're going through, but I know someone who does, and he says you are more valuable than you could ever know."

I wiped my eyes, wondering what she meant, wondering if it could be true, wondering who she was talking about. I didn't have to wonder for long as I began to get the idea as, once again, she placed a hand on the Bible.

"The Bible says that Jesus was a man of sorrows, acquainted with grief, despised and rejected. His friends left him in his hour of need. He understands you, dear. He knows the number of hairs on your head. He will wipe away every tear. He is close to the brokenhearted and saves those who are crushed in spirit."

She stood and poured me a second cup of tea. Now the word "saves" rang out in my brain. The leap into the unknown again. My heart throbbed. The impending explosion was different from earlier that night. It had been chaotic and dark. This somehow had warmth and freedom, like demolishing a teetering old building that was dangerous and dilapidated, only to reveal a spacious landscape of life and a place for growth. The story that Merle was presenting to me felt like a scalpel had been running along my heart. That the hurt and the trial could be cut away—it would hurt, but I would be better for it—and now I knew where to look for the master surgeon; she had patted that Bible too many times.

My tears dried. Merle and I had begun to speak a little lighter when the two men walked in.

"All done," Josh said and placed a warm hand on my shoulder in a surprising gesture of friendship that I immediately read and welcomed. Dad poured them both a tea as they sat with us and Dad explained that the road was cleared.

"And good news too," he looked at me, smiling. "The globes in your headlights were a little dodgy. I had some spares in my shed that suited your car, so I've changed them. You'll be fine to head home whenever you're ready . . . always welcome here mind you!" he chuckled.

I couldn't help but look at him agape. "Wow." I shook my head. "Globes that fit? In your shed?"

He chuckled again. "Even better . . . they are ten times brighter than yours were. They'll really light your way now!"

I shook my head and looked at Merle. Her eyes read mine before I even spoke. "Just what I needed. Thank you. My own light was too dim to see my way. Makes sense if I use a brighter light." I looked at the Bible still covered by my hands. "The brightest light." I paused, and looked back into Merle's eyes. "The only light . . . that I will be able to find my way home."

"And back here anytime," the three of them said together.

I stood to go, and Josh walked me to the door. "Ready to face the dark night?"

I looked down at the Bible I clung to by my side. The storm had quieted for now, but I knew it wasn't over. It would return. I pictured a lighthouse, beaming out its bright light to warn sailors to keep away from the rocks. "The new light will make all the difference," I smiled again, this time not grimacing internally. I was suddenly sure that even the sailors going through the roughest storms would also smile as that lighthouse shone out. I also knew that I would be back on their doorstep. That I had found a support that would be important. My darkness may not dissipate so quickly and easily as that of the night when Josh turned his spotlights on. Mine definitely felt deeper and more firmly rooted. But Merle had spoken some words that were already echoing in my mind, bringing life, leading the way. "Demolishing strongholds," she had said, and I nodded. Walls were beginning to crumble at the message this book contained. I could feel the rumble.

A solitary star peaked out from behind a cloud as I slowly headed down their driveway, easily navigating the potholes, smiling at the vision my high beams now provided.

"Your word is a lamp to guide me, and a light to my path," I repeated. And I knew I had some reading to do.

9

Beyond: A Journey into Prayer

Closed eyes stare in darkness true.
Reality burgeons there. I see you.
Light beheld in its truest form
Carries your heart; kind, welcoming, warm.
Senses speak falsely, but beckon still;
You though, are deeper, beyond reason or thrill.
The air even is fake against your transcendence,
All fades to nought confronting abundance.

    Beyond existence.

And all that you are, before all and in all,
Image of the invisible firstborn over all.
Infinity made by you, all in heaven and earth,
No wealth, power or greatness contesting your worth.
Might beyond armies, present and past,
Impotent time against first and the last.
Never word uttered, no mind could conceive,
Larger than all I can think or believe.

    Beyond apprehension.

Surpassing the finite, outdoing all done.
The earth is your footstool, the heavens your throne.
Higher and grander, truer—and yet;
Stretched beyond fathom, mankind to be met.
Falling so humble to seek and save lost
Bearing the burdens, enduring the cost.
Running the race, in perfection—to win,
Reconciliation, my pardon from sin.

Beyond sacrificial.

You opened the way for me, boldly to come
Outpouring my heart, in your presence undone.
The hopeless empty, enclosed by grace,
Abandoned, surrendered, turned to your face.
You welcome me, soothe and cover with righteousness,
Draw close and attend to all of my frightfulness.
Freely the storm in me pours out like rain,
You rejoice in my joys and grieve in my pain.

Beyond compassion.

Like sunlight you beam as I recount my wins
And cast to the ocean floor all of my sins.
You're tender and jealous with passion for me,
I'm found cradled in your arms lovingly.
The gentle hand reaches, cheeks soft to caress,
You lead and encourage and challenge and bless.
Reminders of promises still true today,
The double-edged sword piercing light to the way.

Beyond truth.

It cuts to dividing my flesh and my soul,
It breathes in me, filling me, making me whole.
With every word uttered or thought turned to you
Your word has the answers, forever is true.
Light to my path and a lamp to my feet.
Successes secret, conqueror of defeat.

Your promises tell me I'm safe and I'm free,
I'm loved and directed and nurtured fully.

Beyond cherished.

You are beyond enough and I conquer in you.
Your grace is sufficient for all I go through.
Your provision is sovereign and constant and right.
Your kingdom sought first brings my soul to delight.
Because you are for us, none can be against,
Your mercy and charity always dispensed,
Peace passing all knowledge in exchange for requests,
Thanksgiving and joy for all trial that besets.

Beyond anxiety.

You raise me and save me and breathe in your power.
You accompany me always, in day or night hour
Your constant renewal by still waters led.
Restored and protected, green pastures my bed.
Goodness and mercy surely attends,
Your kingdom, power and glory no end,
I'll praise you again and again and again.

Amen, Amen, Amen and Amen!

10

Shevach

MITCH HAD MADE IT this far, and he crouched, mentally exhausted now, at the final doorway. Loose strands of hair slipped across his eyes as he stared at the ground, breathing deeply, trying to steady himself—taking stock. Four levels were behind him now, each one more intense than the last, each honing a different skill and drawing him closer to the supreme prize—the treasure of his heart, his ultimate goal: he would finally see his father face-to-face. Everything he had endured seemed to shrink beneath the weight of this moment.

Pressure surged in his mind as he recalled the trials he'd survived and thought of where he was headed now. This game—this life—with stakes impossibly high, had brought him here. At this final level, every skill he'd learned, every hard-won insight and tool, would be called upon. His backpack of supplies sat upright on the ground in front of him as he rested and waited for the challenge to begin. He would need it all, and he would need to summon every reserve of strength and knowledge—and even then, he would face the same relentless foe: the ever-present saboteur.

At each level, it had been the same. He would enter the game cube, and the moment the door sealed behind him, the clock would begin—ten minutes. Ten minutes to gather his bearings, assess the environment, uncover the goal, and devise a strategy. Then the saboteur would be released—free to do whatever it took to throw Mitch off course, to steal victory, kill progression, and destroy any chance of making it to the finish line.

Mitch peered at his backpack, filled with all he'd collected from previous levels—items he deemed helpful, fragments of lessons learned, symbols of hope and determination. He reached in to check his inventory and make sure his mental recollection was sure as he waited for the entry siren to sound.

Each level used a key won in the last round to open the next level's door. He had already retrieved the one inscribed "*Emunah*"—this word written on the door he stood before. He ran his fingers along the inscription and pondered his last lesson.

This word had come to him to symbolize *faith*—not in something distant and unsure, but a deep knowing and belief that held fast, even when everything around him screamed otherwise. He remembered how close he had come to failing that level, and the doubt that had nearly consumed him. He had only made it through that level when he had read some words his father had sent him and had chosen to believe they were true even when the visible evidence seemed contrary.

Mitch sighed as he continued to affectionately stroke the key. He had struggled through every level, barely scraping by, but this last challenge had pushed him to the brink of surrender. He had felt like he was accomplishing nothing, a failure in every regard, stagnant and hopeless. He was ready to walk away—until those life-giving words pierced the darkness. In that moment, the truth cut through the lies, giving him the clarity and strength to keep going. He still had moments of struggling with those insecurities. It was appropriate that this should be the key used on the final door. He needed that faith now.

A calico bag held the other keys Mitch had received, each a reminder of a lesson learned. He pushed it to the side in his backpack and picked up a folder that contained the sacred letters from his father. They were words of anchoring truth; encouragement, wisdom, and direction, and he would've been lost without them.

Not only in the last level where his patient reflection had allowed the weight of the words to settle deep enough within him to absorb the truth in them, but in the previous levels they had helped solve riddles and problems, sometimes showing where Mitch had taken a wrong turn and often giving instruction for his next moves. They would continue to lead to the final victory that he was in this for. The longing of his soul pulsed within him and he sighed again as he placed the letters lovingly back in the bag. The steady sense of his father with him—providing, guiding, leading in countless ways—was as real as breath, but it could not rival the joy of seeing him face-to-face. If he could just make it through . . . he knew that was the only place he would find eternal contentment and safety, wrapped in his father's arms and by his side with nothing to stand in their way. The knowledge of the depth of that bond and communion brought tears to his eyes.

Mitch retrieved a photo of his dad from the backpack. He was a young man in the photo, with wavy brown hair that Mitch had inherited and brown eyes even darker than Mitch's that sparkled with adventure and intrigue. The photo made Mitch smile. "You're an awesome, amazing man, Dad," he said to the picture, and immediately there was a clicking sound from the door and the countdown timer began to ring. He put the photo into his back pocket, cast a quick glance at the other objects in the bag, and zipped it up, flinging it over his shoulder and standing ready. He didn't know what would happen if he didn't make it through this level. The possibilities hammered in his brain. Would he get a second chance? Would he be sent back to the start? Could he lose his very life? He didn't doubt the saboteur's objectives.

The clock above the door that had begun the backwards countdown from one minute reached ten seconds and the final chimes rang out, getting louder for the final three and the siren blast. Mitch slid the key into the lock and turned it without hesitation. The mechanism turned smoothly; every key won had been reliable and worked flawlessly.

Mitch entered, closed the door behind him, and looked around. This cube was different than the other fantastical ones he had encountered. It resembled part of a home. A small entryway opened to a drawing room on the left, and ahead, a staircase led to an upper level.

He moved quickly, sweeping the space with practiced urgency. In the drawing room, he paced a tight lap, brushing his fingers over each object. A tall lamp—switched on, radiating a gentle light, a locked drawer in a narrow desk, a bookshelf, a small, silver trinket box—also locked. A couch with two bright yellow cushions.

Time pressed in on him. He ran upstairs. As expected, the door up there was locked. He needed to find a key. He went back downstairs and launched into a more thorough search—checking behind books, flicking through pages, shifting the cushions. Nothing obvious revealed itself. He stood back to think. His eyes caught the box on the desk and he moved towards it. It had a word etched into its surface; he picked it up and traced the letters slowly with his finger. "*Shevach.*" Next to the word was a keyhole. He didn't recognize the word—but that was no surprise. He had never understood the meanings of the words introduced in each level until he'd lived through the challenge they were tied to. Perhaps "*Shevach*" was more than a name. Perhaps it was a key in its own right—something to be unlocked in him regardless of what physical locks were involved.

He gave the box a gentle rattle; there was definitely something inside. He tried to pry open the lid to no avail. With no other plan in mind, he thought he would try his keys. He put his backpack on the couch and retrieved the calico bag. He tipped all of them onto his hand and clasped them with quiet reverence as the cool metal soothed his damp skin. One by one, he examined them. Each one had once been a mystery. Now, they were memory markers—truths he had been given—freely. earned only by the recognition of some deep truth.

He had received *Khen* in the level where he'd discovered that his own strength amounted to nothing, and that help—unexpected and undeserved—had come from his father. It was his father's *favor* that had carried him through and had never failed, despite

Mitch's own weaknesses. The grace his father always had for him was the strength he needed.

Mitch fondled the next key affectionately. *Shama*, from the darkened maze where whispered words from his father had guided him through each turn. In that place, he had needed to listen carefully to the quiet words and follow through with everything he heard. *Obedience* had been the only way forward.

The *Batach* key was next. It had been a chaotic cube filled with raging waters and jagged rocks. There, bridges dangled precariously above churning depths, crumbling without warning. Each crossing towards the exit was a gamble, some bridges holding firm, while others would give way. Amid the uncertainty, Mitch had noticed something—a faint, almost imperceptible stamp etched into the wood of certain bridges. He stroked the key, recalling the recognition that had sparked within him. It was the mark of his father's building; his father had built some of those components. Reassurance had settled in his chest. If his father had constructed them, they would hold. He had learned a deeper level of *trust* in that level than he had ever known before; wherever his father's craftsmanship was present, a safe path awaited him.

Nothing even came close to resembling *Shevach*—he already knew, still he tried each one. He tucked the keys away again, determined to remember their meaning, to hold on to the truths they carried. But as he did, a soft click came from the door he had entered.

His thoughts scattered. He froze. Ten minutes were up.

He ducked behind the couch as the door creaked open. Peering out from underneath, he saw black shoes—pointed and polished—glide across the floor. The saboteur.

Mitch heard a rustle from the couch and the saboteur turned and ran up the stairs. Mitch's stomach dropped. His backpack. He stood in horror. The couch roared its emptiness into his face. His backpack was gone. The saboteur now had every tool he had earned, everything he would need to make it through. Never before had he lost everything like this, stripped bare, right at the start of this final level. A sick dread pooled in his chest. Should he quit now? What was the point of continuing with nothing? Why go on in emptiness?

He tentatively stepped around the couch and out from the drawing room as he cast a forlorn look up the stairs. The saboteur was gone. Mitch was not surprised. He knew this tactic well. It was part of his skill in deception. Sometimes he was imperceptible, silently weaving chaos behind the scenes—subtly shifting elements, planting traps and unraveling progress in ways that seemed like mere misfortune. Other times he would fully abandon all pretense, becoming brazen and disruptive and striking with reckless abandon, dismantling all stability and ruthlessly set on destruction. He was a master of disguise and deceit and it was one of the things that made victory so hard.

Mitch sank disconsolately onto the couch, the weight of failure anchoring him. With a dull thud, he dropped the calico bag of keys unceremoniously beside himself and bowed his head in his hands. So far, it had seemed simple—find a key, unlock a door—move forward. He was failing so miserably already. Uncertainty swirled around him like smoke. He couldn't even fathom the next step. "I don't feel able Dad," he murmured into his palms, "I feel like I've lost already. I've lost all you've prepared me with, all I've achieved so far. I have nothing left," he moaned and suddenly remembered the photo in his back pocket. He pulled it out and stared at it without moving. Gradually the light that shone from his father's eyes worked its way into his darkness and he leaned forward, continuing to stare at the picture. "You are awesome, Dad," he whispered adoringly, echoing the words he'd spoken at the entryway. A smile colored his darkened face. "I just want to be with you. I love you."

He immediately heard a creak to his left and gazed around. Nothing seemed any different so he turned back to his picture, not wanting to miss the moment as his heart stirred. "You're a great father to me," he sang the words reverently. His voice filled the air like incense, curling upward in sweetness as his heart continued to swell looking at his dad. Another creak rang out into the space, this time much louder. Mitch stood and put the photo back in his pocket and went to the desk, where he could plainly see the trinket box sat ajar, the lid cracked open like a promise answered. His heart leapt and he swooped it up. Inside, nestled like a treasure, was a golden key that looked just like the others; the word inscribed matched that of the box, "*Shevach.*" His heart was pumping and he ran upstairs and tried the key in the door. It opened easily and he peered in.

A long hallway led to a door at the far end. As he entered the hall, he heard the latch on the front door again, and realizing the saboteur was back, quietly closed the door behind him, locking himself in. He turned back to face the hallway, its wall lined with portraits—his father in a hundred different moments. Mitch moved through slowly, brushing the frames with his fingers, drinking in the joy, the strength, the love each image radiated. His chest swelled, his determination for success soared. There were more keys to find, he assumed that much, yet he hadn't even known how he'd released the first one—he'd been singing . . . exalting in his father, caught up in the moment and not even thinking of the challenge.

The hallway ended at a heavy door. Mitch tried the handle but was not surprised to find it locked. On the knob, the same delicate script was clear: "*Shevach,*" but there was no keyhole. He traced the solid metal with his fingers, puzzled, before deciding to put the key securely away with the others and continue searching. He went to reach for his calico bag when the door he had come through shook violently and the saboteur's gruff voice called out from the other side. "I know you're in there, Mitch. I'm going to defeat you, you know." Mitch froze, heart pounding, thankful the door was locked. "I'll wait here for you, Mitch. You can come to me. I have all your keys now, you know." Mitch felt at his side where he thought he'd tied the calico bag and then remembered he had left it on the couch. He gasped and his face contorted as he winced sharply. Nothing was going right. A cold wave of failure slammed into him. The pressure was unbearable. This was worse than ever before. It wasn't sabotage—it was his own mistake; his own stupid carelessness—his ingrown . . . inevitable . . . weakness.

He had personally placed victory in the enemy's very hands. The sting of failure was excruciating.

Mitch ran to the door, shouting as he neared, "My father is stronger than you!" It was the last ounce of strength Mitch could muster, but as the evil laugh of the saboteur rang back, Mitch's resolve gave way.

"I am stronger than *you*, Mitch. I have everything you need. I have your keys. I have taken everything you were relying on. You may as well surrender to me. You know that I am right, you know there is nothing you can do. There's nothing you can give. There's no way forward for you now. You've got nothing."

Mitch staggered back against the hallway wall and sank down to his haunches as his heart cracked like dry clay. The saboteur continued to taunt, "Your father won't want you now. You've failed him. You've failed yourself. No tools. No keys. No worth." The saboteur let his words hang in the air for a moment as they cut deep into Mitch's very identity. Evil ran the knife home with force: "You can't even handle the things he's provided for you. You're not able. You are a loser." The saboteur began to snigger, softly at first, but increasing in volume and pounding in Mitch's brain like it was on loop. The saboteur had won.

Mitch began to weep; deep, soul-wracking sobs. The words echoed, embedded like thorns. The gaping hole of emptiness took hold of him. Everything had led to this and his nemesis was right. He was a loser. He had failed. There was no denying. All he had to his name was one "*Shevach*" key and the photo of his dad in his pocket. He looked up at the photos on the walls. His father's face beamed down, radiant—unbearably kind.

"I can't do it!" he cried through clenched teeth. "My weakness is too much." He hung his head in shame and sobbed deeply. "I'm sorry I let you down. I'm so sorry . . ." His chest heaved in sorrow as the saboteur continued to snigger outside the door.

Mitch took a stammering breath in and released it in a whimper as he looked up, once more, at the photos. He suddenly realized his next key might be hidden in this hallway. He rose slowly, pushing himself up against the wall, fighting with everything he had against the pull of failure. With a deep breath and stifled sobs, he began to look behind each portrait. The saboteur's mocking laughter pressed into his skull like a vice, but Mitch kept going. He reached the end of the hallway in exhaustion, not having found anything, but the images of his father had been subconsciously working magic in his heart. Even as he continued to despair, each one bore down on him like a powerful wave, pushing him forward with both weight and purpose.

At the final frame, Mitch paused, drawn into its depths. His father stood in full medieval regalia, sword raised triumphantly, fire in his eyes. Mitch chuckled faintly, recognizing the old jousting tournament they had taken part in once.

His gaze drifted to another photo. His father proudly holding up his rod, grinning beneath a cap, prize fish dangling close to the lens to make it look bigger than it was. Mitch chuckled again and continued to move down the hall, examining each picture now as there was nothing left to do but look to his father. Unintentionally, even as his tears had continued to silently fall through it all, his smile grew as he looked into his father's radiant face. Those burning brown eyes sparkled out at him in scenes from celebrity selfies to animal encounters—shots mid-laughter or exuding gentle tenderness. A mosaic of moments, each threaded with joy, dignity, and unwavering, unconditional love. The eyes said it all: *I see you. I love you. I'm with you.*

There was no denying it. Mitch shook his head and spoke again. "You *do* love me, Dad. I know it. It's who you are. You are so wonderful." The sniggering behind the door faltered. The saboteur gasped. Mitch retracted his chin in curiosity and cast a momentary sideways glance towards the door, but he didn't care about the saboteur right now; he would not be allowed to steal Mitch's focus. Everything left his vision now aside from the face of his father. There was no game, no timeline, no competition, no rules, no failure, no enemy; just his dad.

Mitch went from picture to picture, commenting on each. "You make me smile, Dad. . . . I can see your love. . . . I love how you love . . . incredible, awesome man." Suddenly the saboteur shrieked "No!" and Mitch heard his footsteps as he bolted down the stairs and out the front door. Mitch blinked and exhaled in the sacred silence. The air itself had changed. Mitch's attention was drawn and he went and let himself back through the door, peering out warily before descending the stairs. He did not know what had made the saboteur leave, but it seemed quite clear that he didn't appreciate the songs of praise Mitch had been passionately proclaiming to his father.

Mitch hurried back to the entryway to check on things, but the saboteur was nowhere to be seen. His situation hadn't improved—still no calico bag of keys, no tools, no backpack—but something had shifted. The cracks in his heart had been filled by the sight of his father's face, like priceless liquid gold poured in to mend broken earthenware. Mitch felt full. His focus returned to the truths his father had taught him; he replayed them all in his mind:

His father's words could be trusted and always had the answer he needed;

He had to listen and follow;

In his weakness, his father was strong;

In dire circumstances, his father's plan could be trusted;

When there seemed to be no way, his father would make a way.

The trinket box lay empty on the desk. Mitch turned to the locked drawer. He pulled at the handle confirming it was still locked. As he pulled his hand away he caught sight of the word "*Shevach*" in the same tiny ornate script engraved on the handle. His heart leapt and he fumbled eagerly for the key in his pocket. With reverence he placed it in the lock; it slid in smoothly, but it would not turn. It didn't make sense. It was the same word. He already had the key. He tried again, and then once more, but the drawer held fast in place.

Mitch took a step back from the drawer, slipping the key into his pocket. He sighed again in consternation and resolve. He had just been rejoicing in how good his father was, at the lessons he had learned, and at the first roadblock he faltered? He shook his head. "I will not be dismayed," he said, smiling. "Just because it looks like it should be the way, doesn't mean it is. When one way seems closed, doesn't mean it is the only way." *When there seemed to be no way, his father would make a way.* Mitch nodded now. "I have no reason for despair if I'm truly hoping in you, Dad." He pulled the photo of his dad from his pocket again as hope surged and his heart swelled with love for his father. Humming the tune he had sung earlier, he clasped his fingers around the handle once more and spoke with resolve as he stared resolutely at the photo in his other hand.

"Dad, I don't know if this is about the key or the lesson—but I'm really beginning to understand—all I need is you. I'll stand and shout your goodness—because of who you are. I know you'll make a way. You *are* the way."

He sang out the words in sweet repetition, "You are the way!" As he sang, the drawer creaked and Mitch pulled gently as he felt the lock give way. The golden key within shone as it hit the light and Mitch retrieved it reverently. It had no pins or cuts on its shaft and Mitch immediately knew it would somehow open the door upstairs with no keyhole. Holding his father's picture close and continuing his exaltation, he ascended the stairs. His voice grew stronger, filled with praise: "There is no one like you. You are everything to me."

At the *Shevach* door, Mitch used the first key to unlock it, passing through the hallway adorned with photos. At the end, he inspected the new key: it too said "*Shevach*," but as he began to wonder how it would work and began to lower it towards the door handle, his song of praise still filling the air, the door swung open on its own. Mitch raised the unused key to his eyeline, staring in awestruck wonder, and stepped through triumphantly into a totally different scene.

Mitch found himself standing on a small platform at the edge of a dark chasm. All that lay in front of him were floating glass panels leading to another door, incredibly—floating on nothing. On the door, a sign beckoned and Mitch caught his breath.

"SUCCESS."

He had made it to the end of the level. He just had to get to the other side.

Mitch glanced below into the seemingly bottomless void. He could not fail. On the wall beside him was a keyhole. Mitch immediately remembered the raging waters in the *Batach* trial, where he had needed to determine which bridges to step onto, and he knew his *Batach* key would have somehow made a way for him here. There, he had discovered the symbol of his father's craftsmanship. Maybe some of these glass panels were his father's handiwork as well. He looked miserably at the keyhole. He peered at each glass panel that led into the distance. He could not study them, he could not examine them closely, he could not know without the key. Despair knocked and began to whisper that all was lost as he remembered afresh he no longer had anything from his backpack of supplies. Everything was gone. He could not pull out his father's letters for instruction or advice, or the tools he had retrieved from previous trials. He could not use his *Batach* key. Mitch drew the two *Shevach* keys from his pocket again and held them high. He turned away from the knocking of despair, declaring triumphantly across the void, "You're teaching me you're worth every breath of praise no matter what's in front of me!" Mitch crouched momentarily as he looked again at his father's picture. He breathed in the strength that came from those eyes. He refueled on the affirmation that came from that smile. He stood and steadied himself. He stared again at his *Shevach* keys before pocketing them with a smile. His father *was* deserving of his praises. He'd sort this out. When he looked at his father's face, nothing else mattered. "Thank you, Dad!" he yelled into the chasm. He recalled now the lesson learned in the bridge trial and the reason the *Batach* key had been won. He knew what he had to do:

Trust.

Jumping onto the first panel, it wobbled but held firm. "You're with me, even when I can't see you!" he declared. "I have faith in you alone!" The clear glass beneath him turned opaque and solidified and the word "*EMUNAH*" appeared on its surface. With renewed courage, he leapt to the next panel. It cracked and shattered beneath him, but he managed to leap to the edge of another, gasping for breath. "I still believe! It doesn't matter what happens. I will trust you no matter what!" he shouted as he steadied himself and watched as the word "*BATACH*" appeared and the panel solidified beneath him.

Suddenly, the door behind him opened. The saboteur stood there with a stupid grin on his face. He held a bag and quickly pulled out a big rock, and before Mitch could see what was happening, he flung it directly at the glass. It fell short of his mark but he quickly grabbed another one and threw again. This time it hit directly on the one in front of Mitch and shattered it to pieces. Now Mitch began to panic as the saboteur went for another rock and continued to throw. Mitch realized he had to move quickly but he had not lost his hope.

"My father once told me to draw near to him, and resist you!" He turned his face toward the surprised saboteur with a steely glare. "I'm going to listen and do what he told me!" he said and turned back, quickly leaping the span of two, just making it onto the next panel. He looked down in enraptured awe as it solidified and "*SHAMA*" appeared on the surface.

"I've learned my lesson!" Mitch shouted as he leapt quickly to the next. "I don't need the key anymore! I can do all things through my father, *he* is enough, he has given me his favor, he loves me, his grace is all I need." "*KHEN*" appeared on the surface of the glass and Mitch raised his arms and burst into song as he leapt again. "You will make a way. What you say is true. There is no one more powerful or beautiful than you!" The saboteur, visibly agitated by Mitch's songs of praise, covered his ears and fled the doorway.

Mitch grinned as he looked down at the final panel which now read "*SHEVACH*" beneath his feet. His heart was swelling in praise for his father, but as he looked at the doorway in front of him "SUCCESS" beckoned.

The saboteur's rocks had shattered the panel that lay immediately in front of the door. A piece of jagged glass hung, wobbling in place, for a mesmerizing moment, then dropped into oblivion. Now, only a yawning chasm lay between Mitch and the door that proclaimed the end. The final step was gone. There would be no cautious approach—only a dangerous leap.

Every proclamation Mitch had just made reverberated through his chest like a heartbeat. There was no alternative. He'd have to jump.

He drew out the photo of his father once more, pressing it to his heart before tucking it safely away, ready to jump. He fixed his eyes on the door, crouched . . . and leapt. Time stretched. The air thickened around him. He reached for the handle, terrified he wouldn't make it—and just barely managed to wrap his fingers around the cold metal. His momentum had swung him hard and he dangled, one arm stretched out, precariously suspended over nothing. The weight of his body tugged mercilessly at his grip, his shoulder screamed. His strength was failing. His own weakness cried out to be acknowledged once again as he hung on the brink of emptiness and success. So close, and now defeated again by his own fragility. Could it be he was a failure after all? After all he had been through?

His fingers began to slip. He swung his free arm to try to secure a better hold and cried at the top of his lungs, "I'm losing my grip!" He missed the handle with his free hand and dropped his head back in despair, moisture from his fingers and palms betraying him. He was a breath away from his inevitable fall, then—like sunlight slicing through cloud—a memory pierced the darkness. Words his father had written to him in a letter once came flooding in, un-beckoned. They came into his mind as sharp as lightning and he realized that even without the written text, those words were written on his heart. Suddenly everything flashed before his eyes. Everything aligned: the trinket box, the *Shevach* door—opening as he sang—without the key, the glass panels clouding over in strength—without the key, and those words filtering into his head without the letters he had clung so dearly to.

In that moment, everything became clear: every door opened, every lock turned, had been through his father's preparation, not Mitch's abilities. His father had gone ahead of him. It had never been about his strength, his own efforts; it wasn't about the keys—it was about trust, praise, and the relationship they shared; it was about love—about knowing his father's heart. In that microsecond he cast a final glance at the sign on the door. Maybe success was not what he thought.

He peered into the abyss that had once terrified him and felt an invitation to surrender. It suddenly shone in a golden light, like morning sun rising over water. He opened his fingers in final abandonment and submission to the fall. As his final grip released, he shouted the words that had come to his mind, with all his might. "Trust and lean not on your own understanding!"

He smiled as he descended into the deep. He fell, and yet—he didn't. Peace surrounded him like wings. There was no fear, only light, and though he was descending—his senses made it feel like he was rising. Memories of his father flooded his mind. "You've shown me who you are," he thought, his heart full of praise. "It doesn't matter if I fall." He suddenly realized, as the pictures from the hallway streamed through his mind, that in each one, his father had a golden key attached to his waist. "You hold the keys! It doesn't matter if I fail, if I lose my grip."

His fall began to slow as all around soft, colorful foliage surrounded him, glowing with beauty. Above him, through the leaves, Mitch could see the game world unraveling. Cubes floating away in pieces; bridges vanished, mazes untangled, locks dissolved.

Mitch sang again, getting louder as each note filled with certainty, "I know you'll unlock it, if it needs unlocking. You said you would open if I came knocking. I know you are true, nothing else matters. You lead the best way, no matter what happens."

Every step, every sorrow, every failure . . . now seen in a new light. Mitch reveled as the whole series of events continued to play in his mind. He had thought he'd lost everything but found he had gained what mattered most. He had tried and failed. In the end, it was not in winning, not in conquering or in knowing, but in worship, in surrender—in his father's unwavering love—the goodness and beauty of the one who called him "son." The whole series of events had been flooded with that reality. Each door that was opened, each lock that needed to be unlocked, was done through what his father had taught him; was done through what his father had prepared in advance. The doors had opened when Mitch had just been in complete awe and wonder at his father's greatness, when he had been focused completely on the goodness of his dad. The saboteur had never had a chance . . . because it never depended on Mitch.

He *did* need to listen. He *did* need to respond. He *did* need to rise and move on. His father always made a way for him to press on. He couldn't have stayed sitting on the couch, he couldn't have stayed collapsed against the wall, but he realized now that his father already knew. The victory had already been written—long before he started. It was in looking to his father that the doors had opened. His father held it all together and this is what had drawn his songs of praise and thereby released the keys.

Finally, his fall slowed, and with a grace and softness that defied the fall, and still filled with songs of praise, he fell right into the arms of his father, who had been waiting at the bottom for him all along.

"I'm glad you let go," his dad said, and held him with all his might.

11

Despair Knocks

Despair knocks.
I brace my back against the door—
a fragile barricade.
Eyes shut tight,
I shout, "No!"

Still, he lingers.
A note slips beneath the crack,
its venomous whisper
curling in my mind:
"All is lost."

I have let him in before,
welcomed him,
believed his words were truth.
Though he wounded,
I called his house my home.

Now he pounds—a thunderous thud.
Tears fall as my hand
trembles on the knob.
He thinks me an easy target.

He has been right before.

He does not relent,
but I have found a better dwelling.
I turn the key,
step back.
The lock holds.

His words are not the truth,
no matter how they seem.
Truth stands stronger
than despair's deceit.
Truth has never left.

Truth is the one who wraps me close,
even now,
as I falter, as I tremble.
Even when I stood in the open doorway,
staring into despair's accusing face,

even when I fell to my knees,
welcoming despair's cold embrace
as though I belonged—
even in oblivion,
even in waste,

still, truth held on,
whispering peace through storms,
strength through weakness,
light into darkness.
Conquering the lies

now I step toward Truth.
Echoes rise around me—
hope, love, peace.
Deep, real, steady—despite the chaos.
I tilt my ear, breathe in.

Despair rages, fists like thunder,

but I have turned away.
I will not answer.
Eyes forward,
one more step toward Truth.

The background din lessens.
He may not stop,
I may still hear him,
but I see clearly now.
Truth calls. Truth holds.

Despair knocks.
I will not open the door.

12

My Father the King
(The Prodigal Princess)

I GUESS THAT PEOPLE on the outside look into my privileged, affluent life and think that I have it all. They're not wrong, but there's more to it. I'm sure many do wonder about life in the palace, but often there's too much of an emphasis on my possessions and extravagant provision. The "stuff" that I have, however, is nothing compared to the position I'm in—whose I am. It's about relationship. Sometimes looking from the outside in, does not give a particularly accurate picture. There's so much that can only be seen from the inside, and so much that, when looked at from the outside, is skewed by the pollution that hovers in the outside air. That is why I write this memoir: to clear the air.

I think my position in the kingdom elicits a lot of judgment; there's so much expectation about my attitude, my demeanor, my responses. And again, rightly so; I mean, my father *is* the king.

To be honest, this life is one of privilege and position that I have to constantly remind myself that I am in. You see the incredible thing that many do not realize is that I was not born here.

I was born a slave. Destined to live and die in chains, just like my parents—scraping by in a system exploited and broken. Abuse and betrayal were familiar. Even within our own, love was twisted into something self-serving and fragile. Poverty and injustice sur-rounded us—just the things this king had always rallied against—the opposite of his ways.

When my parents died and I was left on the street abandoned, discarded like a piece of rubbish, it was the king who found me. He took me in, adopted me, not as a servant or charity case, but as his daughter. His adoption is binding . . . complete. I am his child. He clothed me in royalty and called me his own. There is no privilege I don't have access to, there is nothing that can erase his father-hood. He has deemed me as though I have royal blood flowing through my veins, and what a king decrees is final! My inheritance is from him, my present and future. Sealed and saved. Nothing can overthrow.

Sometimes, the echoes of my past rise up. Lies creep in. I find myself cowering in imagined scarcity and neglect like a beggar, even when a rich banquet is spread before me. It is like I am un-able to partake in what has been provided for me. It is wrong and it is a lie. Some people even try to tell me I'm not his at all. Their accusations sting, but his truth cuts deeper. I have to stand firm on his word. It can be a battle at times and I actually have to forcefully bring everything in line with the truth that has been declared from the highest authority—that I am a princess.

The people outside the palace struggle to understand. They project their disappointments onto the king, imagining how they would run his kingdom better. They misunderstand his love; they misunderstand his ways. I've come to see their blindness with compassion. Vision is so easily impaired. The truth of kingdom life—its richness, its beauty—has been buried beneath misconcep-tions and misrepresentation. It will take people like me, from in-side, to blow the haze away; to bring the message of life and health of the kingdom back to the people. Alas, there is no denying, it is true that even the people from within my father's court sometimes portray things out of line with who my father is, and we cannot blame the outside world for their misguided perceptions.

If they only knew my father.

Sometimes as we travel about the land, I look into the people's faces and wonder what they see as we pass. Some bow and smile, but as I look out the back of the carriage as we pass, I see them carrying on with their day as though nothing happened. I mean, they're not disrespectful, but do they realize who just passed by? I can't help but think if they knew this was the mighty king of all the land, if they knew the love and power he possesses, they would run after us in celebration, they would cry out for time with him. Sometimes the children do—and my father will stop the carriage and scoop them up in his arms for a while as they excitedly blurt out stories and questions until he gently sends them happily along, beaming with awe and satisfaction, and we continue on our way.

I'm continually struck by the deafness that pervades society. From what I've seen, their senses seem dulled by the constant clamor that surrounds them, yet the depth of their oblivion astonishes me. They cling to it as though it were a treasure while rejecting the truth as though it were a blade—sharp enough to cut. And indeed, it can—but only in the most necessary way.

My father will often call out as we pass, showering gifts of love and inviting all to come to the palace, but most stare blankly and pay no attention at all, as if they haven't heard a thing. Sometimes, people will look truly enraptured with the gift they've received but they ignore the carriage as though my father had nothing to do with the giving or as though it was their right to receive such a thing. In others, their disdain is obvious, and I wonder what has happened in their lives that they blame my father. It is as if they purposefully and vehemently reject the notion that it is my father who built the kingdom. *He* knows how it works—he set things up for abundant life and best possible outcomes. He wrote the manual. They toss it aside. I think it's like having a recipe book in front of you, but deciding, instead, to throw in all sorts of poisons and germs of your own choice, thinking they'll add some extra flavor—only to find you can eat, enjoy . . . think how right you were . . . and then suffer the consequences. Only illness and death can come from that choice.

He's the manufacturer, and when we don't read the instruction manual, the machine breaks. We think we know better, but we don't. Following the guidance of the manufacturer leads to perfect use all the time. But again, I consider now that their thoughts can be skewed by the ever-growing external pollution and the best way to get a true picture is to come to the inside, breathe in the clean air, and let the scales fall from your eyes.

If they only knew my father—if they gave him a chance to show himself to them. His constant giving, both blessing and help, to the people of the land is more often than not either ignored or not attributed to him at all. Surely, as I have said, this has to be because of the already ingrained and growing misconceptions and pollution. Honestly, I can't judge them for that; even having had experienced his generous hand in my life, I found I would still forget the source at times. Sometimes that pollution that pervades society hazes all our minds, and we need to breathe the clean air before we gain understanding. I, however, was without excuse. I had come to the palace at an early age, and had seen the character of my father all throughout my growth.

My earliest memory is a time when my favorite wooden horse had fallen from a window to the hard ground three stories below and lost two of her legs. I had run screaming down the stairs to recover her, and without even looking for the missing legs, ran sobbing straight into the throne room. The guards had just stared in bewilderment and let me through, which, now that I'm older, I realize was risky, as my father was in the middle of an important council meeting. I guess, as his daughter, I had authority I wasn't even aware of. I obviously ignored everyone and threw myself into his lap, crying into his shoulder with the broken horse clasped tightly in my little fingers. He did not hesitate to throw his arms around me and stroke my hair comfortingly. I remember hearing the chairs of the statesmen pushed back as they rose in indignation. I heard one of them say, "It's OK, it's his daughter." He carried me tenderly to my room, assuring me he would find Whispers' legs and get her all fixed up. I heard him tell his attendant to let the men know they would reconvene the next day, and I watched out the window as he scrambled through the hedge, triumphantly holding up each of Whispers' legs as they were found before hurrying off, putting the legs back on himself, and then waiting by my bed, where I had fallen asleep in exhaustion, to present her to me with great joy.

There were, of course, other times when my requests were not acted upon so hastily, although he never dismissed me. Sometimes I just had to learn to wait, and it has been my honor to grow with him and learn that though I may not always know why I'm waiting—he does, and it's always for the greater good. Now when I look back and think about his answers, his giving, his generosity, even his apparent delays or lack of an answer, I realize that I had often been blind to his constant provision and ever fervent attention. His storehouses were always open, and he always poured out. It's just that sometimes it wasn't the thing I'd been looking for or expecting and I would miss it. My father knew how to provide, and care, and nurture, and always with such wisdom and love, but sometimes, on top of missing the things he'd given that were right before my eyes, sometimes I saw him not answering in *my* way to mean that he didn't care and that I had to do things my own way; make my own way, prove myself. Those thoughts were wrong, but I didn't know that then.

In my adolescent years, I had grown stubborn and willful and not only doubted the wisdom of my father, but also his kindness. I began to question everything. It wasn't that the questioning was an issue in itself. My father always encouraged openness. No matter what the question or doubt, he was always willing to listen and respond, but I had reached the point of believing more in myself than in him. I stopped listening to him in willful arrogance. I had become like so many of the crowds I had judged before; I believed I knew better—believed I could do better. Looking back on that time, I can see how patient and faithful my father was, but at the time, I couldn't see past my own skewed thoughts to realize how much I was hurting him. Life was all about me. I had been staring out my open window into the unknown, with an insatiable greed and lust growing in my heart. I had been tainted by the pollution of the world beyond. I had let my lungs become accustomed to the contamination, and the addiction it produced drew me like a magnet, away from the purity of the kingdom. Its perilous activity and tantalizing noise called to me seductively. I believed the lies that there were experiences to be had that I had been deprived of. I was invited to partake with no thought or indication of the consequences. I set the furnace ablaze and threw in the tried-and-true recipe book, no longer of value to me. My thoughts were jumbled, my emotions raged, and I felt I could not go on without taking control. I was too proud to surrender and defiantly decided to take the reins.

I told my father I was leaving and insisted he let me live my own life. I am horrified now to think that I demanded money from the treasury as though it were my right as part of the royal family. He gave it to me. Just because I asked. Just because I was his daughter. My demands and denials never made him discount my adoption. I would always be his daughter no matter how far I went, no matter how much I denied him, no matter what I went through.

Even as I left, he was putting my coat on my back and supplies over my shoulders, sending his guards with me down the road for protection. I didn't even realize the extent of his love; I just thought I had a right to everything.

I did look back once as I left. I saw him on his knees sobbing into his hands. I remember thinking he was just being dramatic and not wanting me to have my freedom. My heart had already been calcified by the pollution and my mind was swirling in the darkness. I turned back immediately to the road in front of me that led away from my father's peace and love. I thought I was choosing freedom. I was actually choosing chains.

My father knew the way things worked and desired only for my true freedom and life, but he would not hold me against my will. The decision was mine. My own folly leading to my ruin, and yet my heart raged against the king.

Out there, it seemed vibrant at first. The first taste of the poisonous apple, deliciously sweet and irresistible. I leapt into trying forbidden delicacies, indulging in unexplored playgrounds, swimming in oceans of pleasure, dancing through endless nights. For years I had thought that the outside world did not properly understand us, and now it was I that did not understand them. My delusion steered me down a path I was never meant to take and skewed every thought. The smiles I had mistaken for joy were hollow. The laughter, sharp-edged and shallow. I thought, out here, people found security in their possessions and fulfillment in their choices, but all of it was blanketed in toxic fog. Even in their boasts of accomplishment and pleasure, they could not see the death the poison was bringing. Everything was counterfeit. They did not have a true identity and they did not carry their true worth. I had thrown mine away to join them.

It took a long time for me to see the darkness that lay in the delights. My heart had set hard and my mind was lost. The poison was slowly seeping into my soul and draining the life I had known. It had insidiously worked its way into every fiber like venom through my veins—slow and invisible.

For a time, everything carried on in the darkness with no visible decay. I was enjoying myself, oblivious to the disease taking hold of every part of me. In hindsight, I can see that the poison took its time to make a difference, and I was held aloft by the pleasures that I swam in, not realizing the dark depths below would suck me down and I would be drowned. I, like the people I had previously questioned, became deafened by the noise and blinded by the lies. I squandered the wealth I had set out with. The provisions from my father depleting as I further distanced myself from their source. The associates he had sent for my protection I had long run from—although now I am home, I realize his power and jurisdiction was far reaching, and even in my flight, if they had not held some evil back, I would not have ever made it home. His provision and protection were working and ministering even when I didn't know, even when I shunned it all.

The things I did and became involved with, my deep and growing despair that I was in denial of and was disguised by outlandish actions, continued to trample all over the liberty my father had afforded me and his love that followed me all along my way.

I spit in the face of grace as I reveled in selfish indulgence and ignored the ever-growing depletion of life and repercussions of my choices, little knowing that still—even in the midst of this—he searched for his daughter, he longed for his daughter's return . . .

I was called his daughter.

I had thought I had it all; wealth, friends, pleasure. But they were like cords of death around my neck and as I sank deeper, they pulled tighter and drew all my breath from me. Little by little, everything slipped through my fingers until there was nothing left. I stopped noticing the emptiness, until it filled me. I was drained of all life.

I lost it all.

First, a famine in the land, then financial crisis. I was rotting away with the world around me. My peers began to reject me, subtly at first, then deeply, hurtfully. The ones I had surrounded myself with turned away, each consumed with self-preservation, and a slow, gnawing illness took hold of my body. It crept through my veins like rot, sapping my strength, scattering my thoughts like leaves in the wind. And still, even in my weakness and mental fog, a greedy hunger pulsed in me. I craved more. I believed I was fine—merely running low on resources. I didn't yet see that I was running low on life.

In the aching depths of my soul, slowly, something deeper stirred. A cry—quiet, almost imperceptible—began to rise. It came from a place long buried, but not extinguished, awakened as I hit my lowest point. The lifeblood my father had breathed into me flickered like an ember in ash, and slowly, it caught wind.

From the mire of my ruin, I rose. I resolved to go home.

I imagined—dared to hope—that my father, in his mercy, might let me return as a servant. I could scrub pots in the galley, sweep the floors, earn my keep with toil and silence. At least there would be food, shelter, companions, a place to rest.

The day that I was coming home, I was still oblivious, still blind to how far I'd fallen and how empty I was. With my concrete-encrusted heart, rag-ridden, destitute, dirty and hungry, I struggled to limp along the way. I had no idea how ill I was and how much I had been infected by the pollution I had been living in.

The journey home was a battle. In my mind, voices rose up—memories, doubts, shame—accusing me, mocking me. The very air I breathed seemed to reach out with foul fingers, trying to draw me back to the darkness. I had to continuously fight the urge to turn my back on the kingdom for good. I hadn't realized how much I had forgotten, how much had been lost, but then, as I first caught sight of the palace in the distance, it only took one glance in the right direction for everything to change.

My eyes turned to the watchtower that rose far above the turrets and I could see my father looking out across the land—waiting, watching—and it all came back to me. My life flashed before my eyes and I realized that never once had my father wronged me, never once had he failed me. I crept cautiously closer and watched as he bolted down the external stair and burst with the energy of youth onto the lawn. He pointed this way and that as he ran towards me and soon there were trumpets blasting and horses charging. In all his dignified majesty, I had never seen him run and his urgency to get to me was overwhelming. My heart was swelling beyond what I could bear, but its surge was cracking the hardened outer crust.

I was afraid and stopped in my tracks. I had been given everything, and now was returning in rags, disheveled and broken; I knew this was no picture of a daughter of the king. Surely, he would at the very least throw me into the darkest dungeon for my rebellion and squandering of his possessions . . . and my position. I had let him down. I had turned my back on his love and had believed that I knew the best way to live. Drawn by the lust of my flesh, the lust of my eyes, and the pride of life. I had rejected him in favor of the lies and deceit that only led to my internal demise, and left me crawling home in wretchedness and suffering.

As my father neared, I fell to my knees as the sight of him broke my calloused heart open and my tears began to fall, but as he approached I could hear his sobbing far outweighed even my brokenness. My hard heart cracked wide and bled, and the lifeblood of belonging ignited and roared within. I felt that the drowning in this blood and fire would consume me but I could do nothing but surrender to its cleansing and healing. My father came and fell upon me and swallowed all my anguish in his own. I could feel the poison seeping out of me as his life-giving words flowed and overtook me. "My daughter, my daughter," he could barely form the words, "my daughter was dead but is now alive."

He lifted me up and embraced me fully. I was swept away in his stream of unconditional love. No reprimand, no scolding, no punishment. Never had I been held so tight yet with such comfort.

The horses arrived, and their riders dismounted. My father kept a hand around my shoulder and pointed excitedly, tearfully towards each steward. "Bring me the robes!" and to another, "Prepare a feast!" and to another, "Tonight we celebrate, for my lost daughter has been found!" He took off his royal signet ring and placed it on my finger as I stood shaking. I could not respond. He was accepting me back into his family. He was declaring to me—to all—that I was not rejected, and the declaration echoed so loudly I knew that even the deaf could hear. I knew there would be no galley work for me. His guttural cries turned into a repetitive sob as he fell again onto my shoulder. "I love you, I love you, I love you."

Being held there in his presence, my mind began to clear and I could feel the fog lift. All the years of his loving presence as I grew up came flooding back to me, and I realized how wrong I had been. How he always had my best interests at heart and always had open arms for me, whatever my attitudes, intentions, doubts, or challenges. He had never once acted contrary to his proven faithful and ever-loving character, and even now, in my dirt and abhorrence, had not asked anything from me. He just wanted to hold me and bring me home.

That night as I was brought clean and refreshed to the banquet table and given pride of place, I realized as the king himself held out my chair and seated me at the head of the table that he had purposely laid the table with the Immutz cloth that was used whenever any of his adopted children first received their royal crown. Its deep red material hung all the way to the floor and as he slid me into place I watched my disabled foot slide out of sight at the same time as I felt him place the royal crown on my head. It was an exchange of my self-made disability for freely given royalty and honor. Here I was, carrying shame and weakness, yet through the provision of the king, enabled to shine. He stripped me of my worst and covered me with his best. He had already begun to provide his healing balm that would enable me to walk and breathe in freedom. I could feel it working through me every moment I looked in his eyes, breathed the kingdom air, and tasted of his food. Here I was, loved and seated at the royal table with no doubt that I belonged to the king—washed and welcomed, with an indulgent feast spread before me as though I deserved it. I now knew that there was no facet of deserving. Nothing I could ever do—or not do—or think of myself, could ever change his acceptance of me as his own. Everything before me only came from the fact that the king had placed the crown upon my head and called me "daughter."

Those I had gone to live with—the ones I'd chosen to join—had no experience of this. They believed the lives they lived, the things they indulged in, the choices they made—were the very definition of freedom, but how can one know freedom who has been unaware of their bondage? They had not heard the voice of the one who had offered to show them the best way and to break their chains. The one who had set things in place, knew the right way to live in fullness—in wholeness. He only ever wanted to pour out his love and freedom, and he wanted that for everyone. You see, there is something else I have not told you about my father's kingdom.

It is limitless.

Anyone may come. My father has a huge family—he has a huge kingdom and a huge heart, and never stops his passionate invitations for people to join him. His specialty is the lost, the hurting and the broken; he would always reach out to bring them into his family. He would invite everyone, of course, but they were the ones who, most often, would recognize their need, and respond to his kindness. It was usually the ones who felt they were self-sufficient and were quite capable to manage on their own that were obstinate, stoic, and defiant. They would say they were fine, they didn't need help, didn't need anyone—and as is his way, he would never force anyone, even though he wanted to lavish his love on them; provide them with indulgent feasts, endless gifts, communion, relationship, healing . . . his unfathomable riches. This side of his extravagance went often unrecognized because even those within his kingdom sometimes missed it. Even they thought their primary attention was to be placed on the duties and responsibilities of kingdom life instead of finding those things flowing naturally from their relationship with their father.

I had once looked at my father with my child eyes, seeing no hint of expectation or condemnation. I had been able to run to him and receive his love with no holding back, no shame, no doubt. I'd ruined that by seeping myself in pollution, but he had brought me back. He was refining me, removing the dross, redeeming my purity. I can see him now, not just as powerful king, but as a loving father with arms always open.

He brought me back, even though I was disgraced and had left of my own free will. I had been like a sheep that wandered off and got caught in the brambles, with no way to rescue myself. He had come like a good shepherd and found me, let the brambles pierce him as he delivered me, tended to me and brought me into greener pastures, always wanting my health, my safety, my complete nourishment. I was learning anew that his storehouses were never closed. They were opened to me the moment I became part of his family. Yet it was only from the place of closeness with him that I discovered that. That even now, I can run into his lap as I did when I was a little girl and curl up to be comforted and protected. We can talk for hours and I can sing enraptured in the shadow of his might and love.

Now my soul's delight is to walk and talk with him; hear him speak to me in love and encouragement and direction; know that I am free, loved, wanted, protected, nurtured, heard. I am his.

The wonder of it all is remembering where I came from. His acceptance and forgiveness of me, his inclusion and completion in being part of his family, has been so enrapturing that I can say now, with no hesitation, that I am his blood child. I am overwhelmed that he has pulled me from the filth and mire, that he has called me his own, that he has given me freedom. His life has been injected into mine.

So this is the place I sit and the conclusion of my brief princess memoir, as requested. This is the place for me and for any others who would come. There is life in the fullest to be found here. The invitation is current, and it is passionate. There are many rooms in my father's house. Any may come. If each one only knew him, there would be no question. They would run to him, as he ran to me.

I was orphaned; he is my father. I was lost, but now am found. My name is Nesicha, and I am a daughter of the King.

13

Study Questions

Wastelands

1. Have you experienced a time when you felt like you couldn't keep going? What helped you move forward?

2. In history, peace negotiations were often taking place while the battle still raged. When you are still in the middle of the battle, how might you find encouragement or hope?

3. Where do you turn for refuge? What do you find there that you feel you need? How can you create safe spaces that also help maintain momentum through the day?

4. Like the stink of old cat food, or the stench of rotting flesh, could there be things in your life that are old and rotten and need to be gotten rid of to clear the air?

5. The soldier comments that he needs added vigilance when the enemy is close—to be aware of his presence and tactics. How can you apply extra vigilance to your own life?

6. How does your perspective and positioning contribute to the outcome of your day? How can you use this knowledge to be more sympathetic to where others find themselves?

7. The light in the open doorway indicates a "way out." You may not always see a way out. How can this image draw your beliefs to find hope?

Seasons

1. Considering that one of the beautiful reasons God created seasons was to reflect patterns in our lives, how does this truth affect your belief when you feel like you are stuck in one place?

2. What's your belief about God never changing (Jas 1:17; Heb 13:8)? How can this truth give you confidence?

3. Read Ezekiel 37:1–14. What would you have answered the Lord? Would you have believed the dry bones were too far gone to find life again?

4. God says he will always be with you (Heb 13:5)—how does this affect your belief when you are in the darkness or battlefield? Use your imagination to picture God in the darkness or battlefield with you. What does this image show you?

Free for Freedom

1. The jailer fed the girl. The food was bad but it sustained life. Can you think of things in your life that "feed" you but are not truly nourishing? How can you replace them with something healthier?

2. The girl couldn't bring herself to look to the hallway—she didn't want to awaken hope.
Do you avoid hope for fear of disappointment? How can you explore hope in ways that feel safe and grounded?

3. What sort of things do you put your hope in?
If you are lacking hope, could it be because you believe

nothing worthy to hope in? Do you need to reevaluate? Why/why not?

4. Like the bugs in the skylight—is there something you once found life in that now feels lifeless? What changed? Can it be restored or replaced?

5. Why would the girl think a heart of stone was easier than a heart of flesh?

6. Are there things in your life that are so familiar to you that you press yourself into them for safety or comfort? There are some things like that which may be helpful and good, but can you think of any that might actually be like a prison wall?

7. The prison walls were defeated—door open, no longer holding her—yet she stayed. Why? Do you think you do that? (stay imprisoned when the way is open to leave).

8. As she was overwhelmed and reveling in her own ideas, she immediately forgot the invitation to come that echoed in the darkness. Do we miss invitations? because of the darkness? because of distraction? What do you think your Savior might be inviting you to come to (Matt 11:28–30)?

9. Read Galatians 5:1. The apostle Paul wrote his letter to the church in Galatia because they were falling into old habits and forgetting they had been set free. Where do you see yourself falling into old or bad habits?

Overboard

1. Beauty is not the place for me, the dark and depths "is the place for me"
   What is it that causes you to believe you should stay in the dark when God has seemingly granted light to others?

2. What do you need God to unteach you? What are some of his truths you can use to replace the lies?

3. Thinking of the line "bloodline attaching," what does the thought of a blood transfusion mean to you? What does Christ's blood do for you?

Psalms: A Reflection

1. Where do you see your own experiences reflected in David's psalms?

2. We often see the psalms following the pattern of despair, hoping in the Lord and finally praising him. How could you use this model in prayer?

3. Can you count yourself as righteous? Why/why not? (Rom 3:22–24; Rom 5:19; 2 Cor 5:21) Who will you choose to believe?

4. Do you recognize a battle with an enemy? What can you learn from the psalms about God's reaction and what yours could be? Do you have a mentor or someone you feel safe with? Read Psalm 18 and consider God's defensiveness towards you.

5. Read 2 Kings 6:8–23. Consider or discuss this story.

6. Tearing down strongholds is a concept mentioned in a few of the narratives in this book. How would you describe what this means? Read 2 Corinthians 10:3–5 and rewrite in your own words.

7. Which psalm speaks most deeply to you right now? Why?

In the Driver's Seat

1. How can you be intentional about taking control of your thoughts if you notice them spiraling out of control (2 Cor 10:4–5)?

2. Do you sometimes feel out of control? Is it time to ask for help?

4. Who is in control of steering in your life? Is that working? Why/why not?

5. God is good and merciful. How do you see him showing goodness and mercy to you?

6. Matt drew their attention to the beauty while he navigated around obstacles and into beauty. How do you think God would steer you if you let him?

Fear vs. Faith

1. What are you afraid of?

2. How do you differentiate between positive thinking and faith?

3. Whose responsibility is it to do the work/produce an outcome—yours or God's?
(Some clues: 2 Chr 20:15; 1 Sam 17:47; Eph 2:8; Phil 1:6; Phil 2:13.)

A Brighter Light

1. Driving with the blinkers on—a thought to consider. What does this mean? Do you do that? What does tunnel vision do?

2. The storyteller spoke of carrying the darkness into the night; a futile gesture like the rest of life. Life is not futile (John 10:10). What makes people think life is pointless? What changes this belief? What might not be futile?

3. Josh needs to know where he is going in the darkness. Do you know where you're going?

4. The roads are tricky to navigate in the darkness. How do you navigate?

5. Josh says "I'll show you the way" and "Stick close to me." What can this teach you about getting somewhere you'd like to go—but either don't know the way or the steps to take to get there?

6. Do you try to see things in life through a dim lens? Looking around you, things feel vague and unclear. How might you be able to improve the clarity?

7. There was a tree down on the road, wouldn't have been seen in the dim light, but the bright light showed it up.
   Are there obstacles that come into your life unexpectedly? How would shining a brighter light onto them help? What might that look like for you?

8. Why are lighthouses built? If storms are inevitable and some areas are treacherous . . . and lighthouses are erected for safety . . . why would you not have a "lighthouse" in your own life (John 8:12)? What would that be for you?

9. In the story, a constant, reliable light has been discussed. Do you recognize that what you "see" in your own light might be unreliable?

Beyond: A Journey into Prayer

1. Discuss the themes at the end of each stanza—how can they encourage you? What can they mean for you?

   a. Beyond existence

   b. Beyond apprehension

   c. Beyond sacrificial

   d. Beyond compassion

   e. Beyond truth

   f. Beyond cherished

   g. Beyond anxiety

Shevach

1. Do you have a "backpack" of supplies? Tools you've gathered over your life? What sort of reliance do you place in them?

2. The inscriptions on the keys in the story come from Hebrew and represent some of the tools that God gives to help us on our way. Discuss what they mean for your journey.

    a. *Emunah*—FAITH

    b. *Khen*—FAVOR—GRACE

    c. *Shama*—LISTEN AND OBEY

    d. *Batach*—TRUST

    e. *Shevach*—PRAISE

3. Can you see ways in your life where a "saboteur" works silently in the background—or openly before your eyes?

4. "He didn't doubt the saboteur's objectives." What do you think the father's objectives might be?

5. Mitch wondered if he should go on in emptiness. What was the outcome of moving on?

6. What's your belief about praise? What does it look like to you? How can you let your heart be drawn to praise?

7. What is your belief about success?

Despair Knocks

1. Have you heard despair knocking? What does that sound like? What's your reaction?

2. How can you turn towards truth?

3. How can you know God is holding on to you through it all?

My Father the King

1. Do you feel that people have expectations of you?

2. What might be reasonable expectations to have on yourself based on your position? How can you release the unhealthy pressure to perform?

3. The princess said she had authority she wasn't aware of because she was the daughter of a king. How does this thought fit with your beliefs about yourself?

4. Can you run to God? When you're hurt? Broken? Believe that you have failed?

5. What sort of pollution blurs your mind in your life?

6. Commit to reminding yourself that you are a child of the king. What does this mean?

Help Lines:

In Australia:

Lifeline 131114
Beyond Blue 1300224636
Vision Prayer Line 1800772936
Headspace (ages 12–25) 1800650890
Mensline Australia (for men) 1300789978
Christian Counselors Association of Australia 1300815522

In USA:

Christians in Crisis 1-844-472-9687
LifeChange 1-844-543-3242
Suicide and Crisis Lifeline 988
Crisis Text Line 741741

www.ingramcontent.com/pod-product-compliance
Lightning Source LLC
Chambersburg PA
CBHW072008170626
46813CB00005B/2060